PINEAPPLE DIARIES
OF THE
PEACH STATE

CREATED BY
CHAD WANNAMAKER

Chad W Books

DISCLAIMER

This story is for adults only. It is written to arouse and entertain. Do not read this story if you are offended by explicit descriptions of adults engaging in various forms of consensual sex.

Chapter 1

Exposed thigh in a restaurant was the beginning of everything.

"Damn, she's sexy," Gerald thought, looking across the restaurant at a woman sitting.

Her fully exposed pearl-colored thigh, smooth and flawless, is what caught Gerald's attention. She appeared to be unaware that her dress had ridden up. The sight of it caused a stir in his loins. He had a strong urge to take possession of her thigh, to stroke and kiss it.

Wanting to know who the thigh belonged to, Gerald turned his attention to the whole woman. She had black shoulder-length hair, blue eyes, and a cute nose. Her sundress highlighted her soft, curvaceous, features. They made her look cute and scrumptious at the same time.

Gerald estimated that she was slightly taller than his own wife, Aiko. Her most prominent feminine features were her breasts and her ass. Her thigh, he finally noticed was attached to wide hips and a firm ass. The general effect of her features was to make her look compact, soft and curvy.

She was conversing with a man sitting opposite of her. Their body language suggested to Gerald that they were probably a couple, possibly married. They looked to be relatively young.

"Sir, do you prefer a breast or thigh?"

Aiko could tell that her husband was lost in thought. A light kick in the leg jolted Gerald into the realization that the server had returned.

"Uh, I'm sorry," he mumbled.

"I just wanted to make sure I had your order correct. Do you prefer breast or thigh for the chicken?" she repeated.

"I think he wants thigh," Aiko answered for him before he could utter a word.

The dry way she made the statement made it clear to Gerald that he was, in flagranti delicto. Aiko caught him staring at the woman's thigh. He was embarrassed but then smiled. Gerald knew his wife did not mind his open admiration for other women's physical attributes. She herself was not above admiring other men.

"Yeah, a nice big juicy thigh," he answered, with a smile, while trying to will his cock to soften.

Aiko and Gerald loved each other, but they also had an honest and open relationship that allowed them to appreciate others without fear of jealousy.

What embarrassed Gerald was the thought that someone in the restaurant other than his wife might notice his lust-driven admiration for another man's woman. It was noticeable.

After the server left, Aiko leaned over to get a view of his crotch. She saw that it had gone back to its normal state.

"I bet you'd like to serve that woman some sausage," said Aiko as she leaned back into her seat.

"She is quite beautiful, and seems to be your type. Am I right? You know, cute-as-a button, short with curves in all the right places."

"You got me sweet heart. She has nice thighs, a pretty face, and her sundress does not hide the fact that she has curves in all the right places."

"I guess you used your X-ray vision to imagine what lies underneath that sundress."

"Touché," Gerald answered.

"And what's your opinion of him?"

Aiko licked her lips.

"He's pretty good-looking too, you know."

"He is? I didn't notice," Gerald countered.

Aiko kicked his leg again.

"Okay, okay, he's not bad looking."

"Not bad looking? He's hot. If you weren't so busy staring at her thigh, you would have noticed he caught my attention too."

The man was similar in build to Gerald and appeared to be fit. He had dark brown hair and dark eyes, an aquiline nose and olive-colored skin. Features that stood in contrast to Gerald's black hair, brown eyes, strong slightly bulbous nose and naturally whiter skin. Compared to Gerald's squarish look, this man had a rounder head that seemed to soften his face. Gerald thought he looked like the Mediterranean type.

Then Gerald turned his thoughts to his own wife.

Marrying her, was the best decision I ever made. Although Gerald had had a preference for the type represented by the dark haired woman when he was single, he ended up marrying Aiko, a petite Asian woman with the classic Japanese facial features. While she could be described as skinny before their marriage, after the birth of their two daughters, she had filled out and became curvier, much to Gerald's delight.

Aiko interrupted his thoughts again.

"Now what are you thinking about?" she asked.

"I was thinking about you and our life together. Marrying you was the best decision I ever made," he said sincerely. "No one is more important to me than you are."

"I love you too," said Aiko as she grabbed his hands.

They leaned over the table and gave each other a kiss.

Gerald looked at the other couple again.

"They look like they're having a, uh..." Gerald tried to find the right words, "difference of opinions."

They were too restrained to characterize the animated discussion as a fight. Of course, it was possible that their restraint was influenced by the fact that they were in a public location.

"I wonder what it's about?"

At that moment, the woman said something to her partner that caused him to stop arguing. He looked directly toward Aiko and Gerald and made eye contact. The woman's partner realized that Aiko and Gerald were watching them have their quiet argument. He looked embarrassed. Then he waved with his hand in an apologetic manner, but she still seemed angry about something.

Both couples resumed their meals.

"That's kind of strange. Why is he staring at us all nicely when I'm the one who is being naughty?" Gerald said with a smile.

"I got revenge." Aiko said as she took a sip of her drink.

"What are you talking about, Aiko?"

"While you were thinking your lovely thoughts about me, I accidentally, on purpose, exposed my thigh for him to see. It caught his attention." She said as she smiled, proud of herself.

"A few seconds later, she noticed he seemed distracted and followed his eyes right to me. She got pissed."

"You're a little shit," Gerald chuckled. "Knowing you, I'm sure you were happy with the result."

"It's only fair. You're attracted to her, so I made it my mission to tease her hunk of a partner."

"Well, I didn't cause an argument," Gerald admitted.

Once more erotic images entered his mind. His cock twitched again in response.

A few minutes later, the woman and her partner got up to leave. As they walked passed Aiko and Gerald's table towards the exit, the man apologized.

"Sorry. I didn't mean to offend." He addressed most of his remark toward Aiko.

His wife stood several steps back keeping an eye on Aiko and her husband.

Aiko pretended to be totally unaware of her exposed thigh.

"What for?" Aiko asked.

"Your whole ass was practically out," his wife said from behind him.

"Oh, really?" Aiko said as she looked down at her thigh. "Oh, thank you for telling me."

The man blushed as Aiko adjusted her dress.

The couple then left the restaurant.

Aiko and Gerald finished their desert, a large piece of key lime pie, paid for their meal and left the restaurant.

* * * * *

"They actually seemed like a nice couple," Aiko said as they drove home. "Maybe I shouldn't have done what I did. I got him into trouble."

"Don't worry about it. Maybe she's just the jealous type. And anyway, he should know her well enough to not get caught looking. Rookie mistake." Gerald opined.

"You're an idiot," said Aiko as she laughed.

"It works for us, doesn't it?" Gerald said smiling. "There's no reason why it couldn't work for them. Love conquers all and sex is its lubricant."

"Oh, my god," she moaned, "sometimes you say the dumbest shit."

"Well, if I say the smartest shit, you might not laugh."

Aiko just shook her head at his bland joke.

After driving in silence for a few minutes, Gerald noticed that his wife was thinking about something.

"What's on you mind?" he finally asked.

"Well, something about them keeps nagging me," Aiko said.

"Yeah, what?"

"I remember him. He moved into the house across the street and about four houses down from us last weekend. Remember? The house that was sold about three months ago."

"Really? We've got new neighbors and it's them? I hope it doesn't get awkward when we introduce ourselves because sooner or later, we're going to meet them."

"Let's not wait, hon," Aiko suggested. "Let's just get it over with, go to their house and introduce ourselves. I don't want to be on bad terms with them."

"Okay."

Chapter 2

As they pulled into their driveway, Aiko and Gerald glared down the street to see if their new neighbors were home.

"You see anything?" Gerald asked.

"No looks like they aren't there." Aiko answered as she stared at the house.

Gerald parked the green Denali as he and Aiko made it to their home. He let out a sigh. "Do you think if I were to talk to her alone, that would be better for him? I mean, I can explain to her that there is no reason to be jealous." Gerald said as he leaned back into his seat.

Aiko unbuckled her belt.

"Well, I don't know. She might just be like that. I mean, this can't be the first time it's happened. They will probably be fine. Now, let's go inside so you come inside me," Aiko said with a smile as she exposed her thigh.

"Ohh, sounds good to me sexy."

They made their way into the house, groping each other, and closed the door.

They didn't see their neighbors for a few days. Then, on one warm sunny weekend day, Gerald finally noticed him in the front yard.

"Aiko, he's mowing the lawn. Now might be a good time for us to go over there and introduce ourselves."

"Okay, honey, I'll be right with you. Let me get changed."

When she came down the stairs, she was wearing a white blouse, showing some cleavage, light-denim shorts and her white Asics. Her smooth, flawless legs were accentuated by the color scheme. Her black hair barely reached her shoulders, and it framed her face beautifully.

Gerald wore knee-length shorts and a T-shirt that seemed to mould around his fit body. He was still in great shape for a guy who was in his mid-forties.

With their outfits set, they left the house and walked down the street to meet the neighbors. Gerald was in front and approached the man as he was mowing the lawn.

He stopped the mower as he saw them approaching. To their surprise, the man recognized Gerald and Aiko from the restaurant incident.

"Hello, again. Looks like we're neighbors," Gerald announced extending his hand. "I'm Gerald. Pleased to meet you."

They shook hands.

"And this is the love of my life, my wife Aiko."

"I'm Trevor," he replied as he extended his hand.

Trevor gave Aiko a quick once over, then blushed when he realized that Aiko noticed the glance.

Instead of shaking his hand, Aiko stepped right into him and hugged him as if he were a friend she had not seen in years. This effect on Trevor was immediate. A slight bulge developed in his pants and pressed into Aiko's belly.

"Nice to see you Aiko," he managed to say thoroughly flustered.

"Don't pay any mind to my wife, she can be a tease," Gerald said fully aware of the effect that his wife was having on him.

Aiko smiled sweetly at him as Trevor finally managed to pull himself out of her embrace.

"And now you get to see more of me," Aiko said as she stepped back to reveal her cleavage, bare arms, shoulders, luscious legs and thighs. "Ta-da," she said while opening her arms and hands to show herself off.

"Okay, well, that's nice, I guess," Trevor replied.

"Hey, would you like to officially meet my wife? She's in the backyard doing some gardening."

"Ohh yes, please," Aiko urged.

Trevor led them around the side of the house to the backyard where his wife was planting some orchids. She was on her knees facing away from them, wearing leggings and an old torn oversized button-up shirt. Aiko and Gerald stopped as Trevor approached his wife.

Gerald's eyes took a quick glance at her ass. "Nice, I love those hips," he whispered.

Aiko, nudged him with her elbow, "Down boy. Behave yourself," she whispered back.

"Chloe, we've got some visitors," Trevor announced.

Chloe looked up. She was just as surprised as Trevor had been to see that it was the couple from the restaurant.

"This is Gerald and his wife Aiko."

Chloe removed her gloves and stood up to shake their hands.

The effervescent Aiko moved in quickly. Catching Chloe off-guard, she kissed her cheek.

"Let's be friends," she said without preamble.

She stepped back and then grabbed Chloe's hands.

"You're so cute and sexy. Don't you think, hon?"

"Yes, she is," Gerald said trying to sound aloof but agreeable.

Chloe turned towards Gerald. He shook her hand firmly but yet gently while looking into her eyes.

"Don't be shy. You don't mind if he gives her a hug, do you?" Aiko said addressing Trevor.

Surprised by the question, Trevor didn't get a chance to answer before Gerald went in for a hug. He pulled Chloe into his arms, kissed her cheek and pressed his body against her and embraced her for a few seconds. He made sure to keep some space between his growing crotch and her belly. His instincts told him, not to repeat Aiko's deliberately provocative hug. The couple was shy, and Gerald didn't want to offend them. He let go of the hug, and the two couples talked in the backyard, exchanging small pleasantries.

"Hey, do you want us to give you a hand with this?" Gerald asked, looking around the yard.

"No, we can handle it. We like working outside, sometimes." Chloe replied.

"It's no big deal. Besides, we're not doing anything else today. We were just going to sit around the house, bored. At least this way, we can get to know our neighbors better." Gerald pressed.

"I mean, it is a lot of stuff, babe." Trevor said looking at his wife.

"I don't know. It seems like a lot, and we just met you guys. We don't want to take advantage of your kindness," Chloe responded looking at Aiko.

"We would feel like we're being bad neighbors if we didn't help, just a little bit." Aiko said with a smile.

"Okay, sure. We mainly have to finish prepping the garden, getting the kitchen together, and a few other things." Chloe replied.

Trevor chuckled, "Yeah, by a few other things she means landscaping the front, hanging pictures, and moving the furniture to the 'correct' spots."

"Ohh, that's perfect! You guys can do all that other shit, that I'm not going to help with, and Chloe and I can do the garden and kitchen." Aiko replied with a smile.

"How did I know she was going to say that?" Gerald laughed as he and Trevor walked back to the front yard.

Aiko helped Chloe finish the gardening and set up the kitchen. At the same time, Trevor and Gerald landscaped the front yard and moved furniture around the house. They finished everything except hanging the pictures by late afternoon. After several hours of working continuously in the heat, the couples were tired and sweaty. They decided to call it a day.

"Hey, thank you for the help. We appreciate it. Sorry for being weird about it, but it's been difficult meeting friendly people," Trevor said sincerely.

"No problem man," Gerald assured him.

"We've all put in a lot of work this afternoon," Aiko chimed in. "I don't feel like cooking. Do you?" she asked everyone. Before they could answer, she added, "Let's get cleaned up and go out. I think we deserve a break. Ooh, let's go back to the restaurant where we met. This time we'll sit together and get to know each other better."

"Our treat," Gerald added.

Chloe and Trevor exchanged glances.

"What do think?" asked Trevor.

"Sure, but I think we should treat them because they helped us. It's only fair."

"I agree with her," Trevor said. "We'll go to the restaurant on one condition, that it's our treat. Agreed?"

"Who am I to argue about free food," Gerald said with a hearty laugh.

"Why don't you guys come back over around 6:30 pm? That will give us enough time to wash up and get ready. We'll go together in our car."

"Okay, sounds good." Aiko replied.

At 6:30 pm, Gerald and Aiko returned to Trevor and Chloe's house as promised. Gerald wore his button-up pink shirt, denim jeans, and white Adidas paired with Aiko wearing a short blue dress and white Asics. Trevor wore a polo shirt, blazer, black slacks, and taupe shoes, while his wife wore a mid-thigh pink dress and black heels. The foursome gathered into the car and headed to the restaurant. Laughs and vibrant conversation filled the drive.

Finally, they arrived at the restaurant.

"We had reservations for four," Trevor said to the host.

"Ahh, yes, we have your table ready; please follow me."

As they sat down for dinner, they ordered two bottles of wine.

"What do you guys like? Aiko loves anything red, and I'll drink just about anything." Gerald said with a laugh.

"Let's get one of each then. I don't like red that much, but Trevor loves it," Chloe replied.

They engaged in lively discussions as they drank wine and ate appetizers, waiting for their main courses.

Chole and Trevor were about ten years younger than Aiko and Gerald, in their early thirties. Trevor works as an accountant, and Chloe as a paralegal. They decided that now was the right time buy a house.

Aiko and Gerald have two adult daughters. They learned that their new friends have two sons, one ten and the other twelve. They were spending some time at their grandparent's home while Trevor and Chloe got the house in order.

"Are you guys going to have any more?" Aiko asked.

"No!" Chloe replied emphatically. "It was so hard when they were younger, you know, day care and all that stuff. It was cheaper for me to stay at home with them than to pay for daycare. It's so expensive. Plus, I don't want to sacrifice my career anymore by having a third child. I'm looking at colleges now, planning on going to law school."

"She's the boss. It's not easy caring for young kids. It got easier when they started school, but still. I think for us, two is the perfect number." Trevor said as he took a sip of wine.

"Yeah, that makes sense. We already did that with our two girls. They are on their own, living life. Well, not completely on their own. They still bring clothes home to wash sometimes," Aiko said with a smile.

As dinner arrived, they continued to talk about future dreams and tell embarrassing stories about their spouses.

As Trevor and Chloe split the bill, the group continued to chat animatedly. The four of them left the restaurant together, their laughter blending as they walked down the street toward the parking garage. Plans were already being made for their next outing, and it was clear that they had become fast friends.

Chapter 3

The soft hum of the ceiling fan barely stirred the air as Aiko and Gerald lounged on their bed, the golden glow of the bedside lamp casting long shadows across their bare skin. Aiko lay on her left side, flipping through a travel brochure, while Gerald rested on his back, scrolling through his phone.

"What are you reading?" she asked, absently trailing a finger over the glossy pages.

"A horror story. A couple goes on vacation in Sarasota and ends up being hunted by a serial killer."

Aiko scoffed, rolling her eyes playfully. "And that's relaxing to you?"

Gerald smirked, setting his phone down. "You know me, I love a good scare."

"Yeah, yeah. You and your horror stories." Aiko replied, shifting slightly to adjust the pillow under her head, the fabric cool against her skin. "Why don't you read something sensual for a change?"

"You mean like that one book about aliens having sex with a couple in bondage?" he teased, rolling onto his side to face her.

She raised an eyebrow and couldn't help but laugh. "Not exactly what I had in mind, but now I'm curious." She admitted, her interest piqued by the absurdity of it all.

The atmosphere shifted as they shared a moment of laughter, the playful banter igniting a spark between them. It was a reminder that they could weave their own stories together in their cozy sanctuary, whether they were thrilling, romantic, or delightfully absurd.

Gerald slid closer, his hand trailing over the curve of her hip before gliding up to cup her breast. His fingers brushed her nipple, teasing it to a firm peak before he reached across to claim the other. Aiko exhaled softly, feigning interest in her brochure a moment longer before surrendering to the sensations his hands stirred.

"Mmm," she purred.

But she wasn't ready to lose herself entirely just yet.

"What do you think?" she asked, voice husky.

"About what?" He didn't stop his slow, lazy exploration.

"Our new neighbors."

Gerald's hand hesitated for just a second before resuming its caress. "Chloe's sexy. I don't think she realizes just how much."

"Do you want her?"

"I mean, yeah. I'd fuck her in a heartbeat."

Aiko bit her lip. "Trevor's not bad either. I wouldn't mind having him in my bed."

Gerald chuckled, rolling onto his back as she playfully jabbed an elbow into his ribs.

"Ow."

"Ohh, please, that didn't hurt. Feeling abused, sir?"

"Not at all." His grin turned wicked. "But I can abuse that ass of yours."

She arched her back, pressing against him. "This ass is all yours, babe. Do what you have to do."

His hand slipped lower, fingers finding the heat between her thighs. He groaned as he discovered just how ready she was.

"That for me, or are you thinking about Trevor?"

Aiko turned her head, lips grazing his ear. "You," she whispered.

Gerald nipped the sensitive skin beneath her jaw, his other hand kneading her breast. "You think we should make a play for them?"

"Yes," she sighed, shifting against his touch. "But we'll have to go slow. We don't want to scare them off, especially Chloe."

Gerald hummed in agreement, but words soon became unnecessary. His fingers explored her with practiced ease, teasing, stroking, pressing into the velvet heat of her center. He brought them to his lips, tasting her, his eyes dark with hunger.

Aiko gasped as he replaced his fingers with his erect rod. He began by teasing her with shallow thrusts before sinking deep inside of her.

For a long while, nothing else in the world existed. Only the heat between them, the rhythmic push and pull, the way their bodies moved together like a well-rehearsed dance. Aiko clenched her toned pelvic muscles around his stiffness, and Gerald groaned, burying his face against her shoulder.

"You drive me crazy when you do that," he panted. "I don't want to come too soon."

"It's okay," she whispered. "I'm close, too."

With that, Gerald surged forward, thrusting deeper, faster, chasing the peak that hovered just out of reach. The feeling mixed with her aroma elevated his arousal.

Aiko shattered first, crying out as pleasure ripped through her. Gerald followed, his release spilling into her, mingling with the warmth already between them.

They lay there for a moment, tangled in each other, their bodies slick with sweat and satisfaction.

Finally, Gerald exhaled a breathless laugh. "I think I got a cramp from that one."

Aiko smirked, stretching. "Worth it, though."

"Definitely."

Aiko got up and went to the bathroom while Gerald wiped off with his old shirt and changed the sheets. Aiko's waterfall had drenched the bed.

They got back in bed after cleaning up. Gerald pulled Aiko against him, spooning her as they settled in.

"Hold me," she murmured.

"Always."

Gerald's breathing evened out, but Aiko's mind still buzzed. She let her hand drift down, stroking him lightly. His soft grunt told her he was barely awake.

"Do me a favor?"

"Mmm?" Gerald grunted back awake.

"Think about Chloe."

His body tensed for a fraction of a second. "Why?"

"Just do it," she coaxed, squeezing him.

Gerald sighed, shifting slightly. "Okay, okay."

As he let his mind wander, she stroked him to life again. Once he was fully hard, she grinned, shifting to straddle him.

"Figured thinking about her would do the trick," she teased.

"You figured, did you?" Gerald said with a smile.

His hands gripped her hips as she sank onto him, rolling her hips in slow, deliberate movements.

Aiko moaned, tossing her head back. "I'm going to think about Trevor now. About how good he would feel inside me."

Gerald groaned. "Damn. That's hot."

"So hot," she breathed, moving faster. "This is our little virtual swap."

"Virtual swap?"

"Mmm, I'm your avatar for Chloe. You're my avatar for Trevor."

Gerald groaned again, gripping her tighter. The idea of it, the fantasy, only fueled the fire between them. They moved together, chasing another climax, surrendering to the thrill of shared desire. Aiko switched to reverse cowgirl and continued her rhythmic bounce on top of Gerald.

He loved seeing sweat roll down Aiko's arched back.

"Yes, yes. Don't stop, babe." Aiko called out, almost breathless. "Fill me up again. I'm ready for you."

Grunts filled the steamy room as Gerald heaved into her.

"I'm about to cum!" she called out.

"Me too!" Gerald let out with a loud grunt.

They both exploded in a climactic finish, soaking the sheets again.

Aiko collapsed backward onto his chest, breathless.

"That was some good shit," she squeaked out.

"Yeah, good thing we have that plastic bed cover," Gerald muttered.

She laughed, rolling off him. "Best Costco purchase ever. Clean up on aisle three, please," she laughed.

"Yeah, I'll grab the sheets again," Gerald announced as he wiped off with his shirt again.

Back in bed after another cleanup, Aiko snuggled against him. They relaxed in the afterglow of their most recent session. Several minutes later, Aiko broke the silence.

"You really think we can seduce them?"

Gerald yawned. "I don't think we read them wrong. I just think they need a little... coaxing. I mean if they are adamant about not doing it, then we just have some new sexy friends."

"Yeah," Aiko murmured, already plotting.

Gerald, exhausted, was out within minutes. Aiko followed soon after, her dreams filled with dark eyes, forbidden hands, and the promise of something new.

Chapter 4

As the weeks passed, the two couples grew closer, their initial awkwardness fading into easy camaraderie. Weekend cookouts, game nights, and casual gatherings became routine. The connection between them felt natural and effortless until an unexpected conversation shifted the dynamic.

Aiko and Gerald invited Trevor and Chloe over to watch a baseball game one Sunday afternoon. When they arrived, Gerald greeted them at the door with a grin.

"Hey, guys, come on in. Aiko's in the kitchen getting the food ready, and the game's just in the second inning, so you didn't miss much."

"You two go watch the game, and I'll help with the food," Chloe said, making her way toward the kitchen.

As she stepped inside, the scent of sizzling appetizers and warm spices filled the air. Aiko stood at the counter, focused on arranging a platter of snacks. She glanced up at Chloe and smirked.

"I think the Braves are already losing," Aiko quipped.

Chloe rolled her eyes as she grabbed a chip and dipped it into the bowl. "They really love their baseball. I don't get it. It's okay in person, I guess, but watching it on TV? I'd rather watch paint dry."

Aiko hesitated for a moment, her fingers gripping the edge of the counter. When she finally spoke, her voice was softer and more deliberate.

"I've got a confession to make."

Chloe arched a brow, intrigued. "Ohh? Scandalous? What is it?"

Aiko bit her lip. "I'm worried you might get mad at me."

Chloe stilled, her amusement fading into curiosity. "I promise I won't get mad. Just tell me."

Aiko inhaled deeply, then met Chloe's gaze. "Do you remember when we first saw each other at the restaurant?"

"Yeah..."

"I sort of... showed my 'Thass' to your husband on purpose."

Chloe blinked. "Wait. You did what now?"

"My thigh and ass crease," Aiko clarified, her voice barely above a whisper.

A stunned silence stretched between them. Then Chloe's eyes narrowed. "Why the hell would you do that?"

"Wait, let me explain!" Aiko rushed out. "I know it sounds weird, but I didn't mean any harm. I wasn't thinking."

"Okay, Aiko. Explain. Now."

Aiko exhaled, shifting uncomfortably.

"Gerald noticed you first. He pointed out how good you looked. Then I saw Trevor watching you, too. It was all playful. I was just teasing my husband. I didn't think it would matter."

Chloe crossed her arms, her pulse kicking up.

"I did not have my ass out. I'm not like that, like you, apparently."

"I know that now," Aiko said quickly. "But we didn't know each other then. It was a silly, impulsive thing. I just wanted to tell you because I still think about it sometimes."

Chloe stared at her, emotions warring inside her—irritation, disbelief, and something else. Something unexpected.

"We had an argument because of that shit. What the fuck is wrong with you? And Gerald, just what? He went along with it?"

Aiko shrugged. "He understood what I was doing. It wasn't a big deal to us. He saw you, thought you were hot, and I just... played along. It was nothing."

"Wait. Gerald thinks I'm hot?"

Aiko's lips curled into a knowing smile. "Of course he does. Trevor does, too."

Chloe's cheeks burned. She looked away, suddenly aware of the tension crackling in the air. "I... didn't realize that."

"Does that bother you?" Aiko asked, her voice smooth and measured.

Chloe hesitated. "I mean... I guess not."

"So, do you think Gerald is attractive?" Aiko pressed.

Chloe's breath hitched. "I—I haven't really thought about it. I guess so."

"You guess so? What is that shit?" Aiko laughed.

Chloe exhaled sharply. "Okay, fine. Yes. I do."

"Is he sexy?" Aiko whispered, a teasing glint in her eyes.

"Yes. He is."

"But you still love Trevor, right?"

"Of course I do."

Aiko grinned triumphantly. "Then there you go. Loving your husband doesn't mean you can't find someone else attractive."

Chloe let that thought settle, rolling it over in her mind. It made sense. Didn't it?

Aiko leaned in, lowering her voice.

"One more confession."

Chloe groaned. "Ohh my god, what now?"

Aiko's lips curled at the corners. "I think your husband is very sexy. We're lucky to have such gorgeous men, don't you think?"

"I mean... yeah, I guess." Chloe hesitated. The words should have made her uncomfortable, but they sent a strange thrill through her.

"We love our husbands, but we notice other people. So what if they do, too? They only love us."

Chloe couldn't argue with her logic.

Aiko glanced at her watch. "We've been talking for twenty minutes. The guys must be wondering what's taking so long."

They grabbed the food and returned to the living room.

"What were you two up to?" Gerald asked, throwing a glance their way.

"Girl talk, honey," Aiko answered sweetly.

Gerald smirked. "Well, you missed a home run. He smacked it so hard I thought it was going over the left field wall."

"Ohh, sorry I missed that," Aiko teased. "Maybe they'll hit another one and actually win this game."

Gerald shot her a blank stare before returning his focus to the screen.

As the game wound down, Chloe stretched. "We've got to go. Need to pick up the kids."

"Thanks for coming over," Gerald said. "See you soon."

After Trevor and Chloe left, Aiko turned to Gerald, her expression thoughtful.

"So... do you think they'll be into it?" Gerald exhaled.

"Hard to say. She was tough to read. She got mad when I told her what I did though." Aiko bit her lip. "Whatever happens, the timing has to be right."

Gerald smirked. "Let's push things a little. Be a little extra friendly."

Aiko gave him a warning look. "We have to be careful. We don't want to push too hard. If nothing happens, I'd rather have them as friends. They're good people."

Gerald nodded. "Agreed. But something tells me... this is just the beginning."

Chapter 5

Chloe and Trevor had long noticed that Aiko and Gerald were occasionally absent on weekends. They assumed their friends were visiting their daughters or other family members. Other times, Aiko and Gerald had overnight guests—some family, others who were clearly not. Strangely, the non-family visitors were never introduced, despite the fact that Aiko and Gerald had willingly introduced them to other friends before.

Chloe and Trevor exchanged curious glances but chose not to pry. Their friends had their reasons, and they left it at that.

What they didn't know was that Aiko and Gerald had a plan—a carefully calculated one. They saw Chloe and Trevor's birthdays as the perfect opportunities to grow closer, to push boundaries just enough to test the waters. The key was improvisation, adapting to the moment as it unfolded.

Chloe's birthday came first.

Gerald was dressed in a pair of blue Izod golf shorts and a pink T-shirt, casual but intentional. Aiko chose a short red-and-white skirt with a crisp white blouse, leaving the top button undone just enough.

As they approached their neighbor's house, Aiko gave Gerald a playful nudge. "Make sure you give Chloe a nice hug and kiss," she murmured. "Since we're together, it won't seem that unusual."

Gerald chuckled, adjusting his shirt. "Yes, ma'am."

They reached the front door, rang the bell, and waited.

Trevor opened it with a warm grin, sweeping his arm in welcome. "Come on in, guys. Chloe's upstairs; she should be down in a minute."

The three of them moved into the living room, settling onto the couch. Light conversation filled the space as they waited. Moments later, the soft sound of footsteps on the stairs signaled Chloe's arrival.

As she came to the bottom of the stairs to the left of the living room, Aiko jumped up, walked over, and gave her a hug and a kiss on the cheek. "Happy Birthday, Chloe."

"Thank you," she replied with a smile.

Chloe was about to offer her cheek to Gerald as he was now up and walking over, but instead, he surprised her by wrapping his arms completely around her and then giving her a firm lingering hug. Then he kissed her on the cheek, near her neck. Feeling her body against him, her soft skin, and the scent of her perfume caused his penis to stiffen.

Although only a few seconds passed, Gerald held onto Chloe just long enough for her to detect the unmistakable bulge in his pants. Too stunned to react, Chloe did not immediately push herself off from him. Instead, she almost found herself responding to his kiss. She felt a bit naughty, and excited. The tingling between her legs an apparent response to his unexpected embrace.

Before she had a chance to recover her sense of propriety, Gerald let her go. The flicker of both excitement and embarrassment that he had seen in her eyes told Gerald that his embrace achieved the desired effect.

When Chloe looked into Gerald's face, she saw attraction and lust in his eyes. She knew that Gerald was attracted to her. Aiko had told her so. But she suddenly realized that he lusted after her. And she enjoyed it. His physical reaction to her flattered her and made her feel sexy.

Then her mood changed as embarrassment quickly replaced flattery. Then a sense of guilt entered into the mix of her emotions.

"I shouldn't feel like this about her husband." She thought that her unbidden physical reaction to Gerald's hug and kiss was inconsistent with her vows. She was sure that she loved her husband. But it still felt wrong to be so sexually attracted to another man. Her feelings were in turmoil, and she struggled to keep it hidden.

Gerald was discreet. He smiled with a twinkle in his eye but otherwise pretended that nothing out of the ordinary had happened.

Trevor just interpreted what he saw as a display of extra affection for Chloe because it was her birthday. But he also noticed that his wife looked slightly flustered. When he looked to Aiko, she seemed to behave as if nothing untoward had happened, so he ignored it.

"I should get some snacks for us." Chloe said as the awkwardness passed.

She was desperate for an excuse to be alone for a few moments to regain her composure. She needed to get her sexual reaction to Gerald's sensual hug under control. She did not want Trevor or Aiko to guess that Gerald had excited her. She hastily walked to the kitchen.

"Well that was kind of weird," Trevor thought.

"I'll go get us some beer then," Trevor told Gerald as he followed his wife to the kitchen.

"What's up?" he asked in the kitchen. "You're acting a little strangely."

"I'll tell you later," she said in a tone that told him that now was not the time to press the issue.

"Okay. Sure." Trevor said in a flat tone. But he thought, "I'd swear she's looking guilty about something."

Meanwhile, with both Chloe and Trevor in the kitchen, Aiko and Gerald had a few moments to themselves.

Aiko gave her husband a wink. "Good job," she declared, "Now it's my turn."

When Trevor returned with two beers, Gerald and Aiko were sharing the sofa, sitting next to each other. He handed a beer to Gerald.

"Thanks buddy," Gerald said, "I can use a beer to cool down."

Trevor saw the wisp of a smile quickly develop on Aiko's face and then almost as quickly disappear.

"Am I missing something?" he asked. "I mean it is a little warm, but not too hot right?"

"No, it's fine. I was just making a terribly lame joke."

"Ohh, yeah dude, that was pretty trash," Trevor said with a laugh.

Trevor sat in the chair at the short end of the coffee table. "Cheers," he said to Gerald as they tapped their beers together.

"I'll check on Chloe to see if she needs any help," Aiko said as she stood up. "You guys just talk about boring guy stuff anyway. Enjoy your beers." She headed for the kitchen.

As Aiko walked into the kitchen, she said, "Ohh, it's a little hot in here, isn't it?"

"The air circulation isn't as good as it should be," Chloe acknowledged, "Especially after cooking."

Aiko loosened the second and third buttons of her blouse. "That should help," she said aloud, seemingly to herself. "Would you like me to bring some snacks to the guys?"

Chloe saw that she she had now exposed more flesh although the blouse still covered her breasts. Aiko was not wearing a bra, and she had firm perky breasts.

"Sure, right over there." Chloe pointed at the counter. She sighed with relief because she did not want go into the living room yet. She needed time to regain her complete composure.

Aiko picked up two bowls, one with street tacos and the other with guacamole dip, then returned to the living room.

"It's hot in the kitchen too," she commented to the men. She waved her hand in front of her face as if to fan herself.

Gerald noticed that she now had undone three buttons of her blouse. He had a pretty good idea what she was about to do.

She stooped in front of Gerald, putting down the bowl of tacos on the coffee table. The angle enabled him to see inside her blouse. He immediately saw her breasts dangling down inside her blouse. His mouth watered at the fleshy sights. He was tempted to put his hand inside her blouse and play with her firm womanly mounds.

Given that Trevor was sitting at a 90-degree angle, he noticed nothing unusual other than what seemed to be a harmless flirtation taking place between a wife and her husband.

Gerald, of course, saw much, much more. He looked in his wife's eyes and smirked. She had just let him in on her plan. She put the bowl of tacos on the table.

Gerald watched as Aiko stood up again, stepped across in front of him and then turned to face Trevor. She stooped to put the bowl of guacamole dip in front of him.

"Here are some more treats," she said smiling.

Gerald almost guffawed at Aiko's cheeky humor.

Trevor's eyes widened. He had a clear view of Aiko's two beauties dangling inside her blouse.

"I hope you're hungry," she said sweetly, pretending not to notice her partially open blouse.

Trevor barely heard as his eyes were glued to Aiko's adorable breasts. They were slightly smaller than Chloe's, but firm, and were shaped like mangos, whereas Chloe's were rounder. But they certainly looked delicious. He wanted to put one of them in his mouth, to taste and savor it, and then sample the other one too. He wondered what it would feel like to draw his tongue across one of her beautiful nipples. He was even more enraptured when he saw the nipples harden.

His gaze felt like strokes, making her nipples stiffen. Aiko stood still for a few seconds while holding the guacamole dip. She didn't want to distract Trevor by making a movement. She knew what was going on in his mind. The man's obvious look turned her on.

Trevor gulped. He was almost mesmerized.

Finally Aiko put the dip on the coffee table. The sound broke Trevor's focus.

She stuck her finger in the dip and put it in her mouth.

"Hmm, delicious," she said.

"Uh, yeah," he grunted, and then suddenly realized that the owner of those two lovely breasts was talking to him. He turned red. "Ohh, I'm so sorry," he blurted out. "I didn't mean to..."

But Aiko interrupted him. "Yes, you did," she said smiling. "Don't worry about it," she said gently. "The guacamole dip really is delicious, you know." She giggled.

Trevor blushed again because when he first heard the word 'delicious' it was the word that flashed through his mind when his eyes were filled with Aiko's tits.

Suddenly, he remembered Gerald. He turned to him and saw him laugh. He was relieved because for a split second he thought he was going to get a fist in his face.

"My fault," Aiko said as she buttoned up the second and third buttons. It was hot in the kitchen. "I was just trying to keep cool."

"Yeah, right," Gerald snickered, "All you did was bring the heat to the living room."

"Don't be crude, Gerald," Aiko pouted and smiled at the same time.

Roughly ten minutes later, Chloe returned to the living room with additional snacks.

Although the rest of the evening among the four of them proceeded normally enough, inner turmoil nagged both Chloe and Trevor.

As for Aiko and Gerald, they were happy with the result. They had managed to push their friend's boundaries. They had finally opened the door to something more without getting it slammed in their faces.

Chapter 6

After Aiko and Gerald left, Chloe couldn't shake the guilt gnawing at her. Gerald's hug lingered in her mind, making her stomach twist with unease. Hours had passed in their company without another incident, but the moment still felt like a weight on her chest. She needed to tell Trevor.

If I don't tell him and Gerald lets it slip, Trevor might think I was hiding something. He might not trust me anymore.

She stole a glance at her husband, who sat beside her on the couch, relaxed and oblivious. The thought of keeping it to herself made her anxious. Taking a breath, she blurted it out before she lost her nerve.

"Babe, I think Gerald made a pass at me."

Trevor turned to her, his brow lifting in mild curiosity. "Oh really? When? You know he likes to flirt."

Chloe hesitated. "When he hugged me."

"I saw him give you that extra-long birthday hug, but I didn't notice anything else. Did he do something when I wasn't looking?"

She exhaled sharply, frustration creeping into her tone. "You were looking. You just didn't see."

Trevor frowned. "What do you mean?"

Chloe squared her shoulders, meeting his gaze. "I'm not the most experienced woman in the world, and maybe I'm a little naïve, but I know an erection when I feel one."

Trevor blinked. "What? Are you sure you didn't imagine it?"

Her jaw tightened. "Imagined it? That was no imaginary cock pressing against my belly, babe. And I think he knew exactly what he was doing."

Trevor stared at her, caught off guard by her bluntness. Chloe, usually measured with her words, had left no room for misinterpretation.

"If Aiko pressed herself against you, what do you think would have happened?" Before he could answer, she added, "I know what, you'd get a hard-on too. Wouldn't you? I know you, you, you asshole! I know you're attracted to her."

"I haven't..." he started to say, but Chloe cut him off.

"Been unfaithful?" she completed. Then she softened. "I believe that. I don't think you've ever cheated on me. I just want to make sure you know I won't cheat on you." Then a streak of jealousy shone through. "But an attractive woman like Aiko could certainly get a rise out of you."

"Okay, you got me. It's true that she's attractive, but I love only you." His priority was to reassure her.

She seemed to accept his forthright answer.

"At least he's not trying to deny the obvious," she thought.

Her reaction to the entire situation made Trevor wonder if there were more to the story. If what happened was the whole story, he was fairly certain that she would have just brushed off the incident as a momentary and spontaneous indiscretion on Gerald's part. She would then avoid similar situations with Gerald in the future.

Then a thought occurred to him, a thought that might explain his wife's guilt and her subsequent statements toward his attraction to Aiko.

"Did you, get turned on too?" he probed.

"I wouldn't..." she stammered, but her blush was her confession.

"Ohh, so something else happened. What?"

Chloe blushed but didn't respond.

"What happened babe?" he asked again.

"Okay! Okay." She took a deep breath and continued. "Well, when I felt his, his... hard dick against me, it turned me on a little." Then she began to tear up. "I'm so sorry, Trevor," she cried.

"No wonder you're feeling so guilty," he replied.

Trevor felt oddly relieved at her confession. He realized it would help take him off the hook when he made his own confession.

He hugged and kissed her.

"It's okay," Trevor assured her. "It's not that big of a deal."

He saw some doubt flash across her face.

"We are married and love each other. In fact, I think it would be almost unnatural if we weren't at least occasionally sexually attracted to someone else. So don't worry about. What we have between us is special and unique to us. That's what counts."

Chloe was visibly relieved although she noticed that Trevor had used the same argument as Aiko. But then again, she had herself acknowledged this truth.

"Thanks babe," she said wrapping her arms around him and then tilting her head back to kiss him. Allowing her flowing hair to fall behind her shoulders. "I needed to hear that vote of confidence."

"The important thing is that we're honest with each other." He decided that now was the time to make his own confession. "Besides," he added, "We're on equal footing. I found myself in a similar situation tonight."

"How so?" she asked looking up into his eyes.

"Well, you know Aiko went to the kitchen and brought back some snacks. Right?"

"I remember. She offered to help. I asked her take some snacks to the living room for you guys."

"Right. When Aiko came back," he continued, "She put the tacos down on the coffee table in front of Gerald. When they looked at each other, there was that funny all knowing look in their faces as if they were signaling to each other about something."

"A knowing look? What do you mean?" she asked.

"Well, I soon found out," he said with a chuckle.

"And..." she said forming circles with her fingers to encourage him to continue.

"When she bent over to put the guacamole dip on the coffee table, I got an eye full of her tits."

"No way!" she exclaimed. "When she was with me in the kitchen, she undid a couple of buttons because, she said, it was hot in the kitchen."

"She knew I was staring at them too," Trevor continued. "She made fun of me for it."

"Made fun of you?"

"Yeah, because she showed off herself to Gerald first. I saw him smile."

"And Gerald just watched?" she said in amazement.

"Watched? He laughed as if it were a big practical joke."

"You got to be kidding. Maybe you just read the situation wrongly."

"Yeah... right. I don't think so," he said. "She made no effort to cover her tits once I saw them. I swear she jiggled them for a second too. Then she looked me in the eye and smiled."

"Wow." she said.

"Call me stupid, but if I didn't know any better, I'd swear they were both in on it and were coming on to us."

Chloe looked at her husband in disbelief.

"What other explanation is there?" he declared.

"I mean I guess, maybe they have that type of lifestyle where they tease people to make their sex lives better. I saw it on a Bravo show." She replied.

"Well, we should just tell them that we're not like that. We like being friends, but not flirting like that."

"Okay babe, I like the sound of that."

Later that night, Trevor was in his pajamas playing a game on his tablet while Chloe was in the shower. He was so into his game that he did not notice Chloe come out of the bathroom until he felt the motion of her settling herself on their bed next to him. Suddenly, Chloe reached into the fly of his pants and pulled out his flaccid cock. She put it in her mouth and sucked urgently.

He put his tablet aside. There was no way he could concentrate on the game now. This was better than anything the tablet could offer. Chloe was totally nude, and the look of her smooth skin, speckled with red patches from the hot shower increased his arousal. The smell of her lavender soap filled his nostrils. He breathed her in.

He became erect in seconds. His mind switched from the game to his sexy naked wife. He realized that the erotic high he had derived from seeing Aiko openly flaunt her breasts still lingered in his psyche. Usually, it was Trevor that initiated sex, but Chloe had caught him by surprise. She had taken the initiative. He surmised that Chloe could still be feeling the after-effects of Gerald's sensual birthday greeting. He also realized that he was more than happy to accept the benefits.

"Easy, babe, or you'll make me finish in your mouth."

She stopped. She wanted to feel his hard rod in her.

Trevor quickly took his pants off.

"Come here." He patted on the bed inviting her to sit right next to him.

When she settled in, he put his arm around her shoulder and then drew her to him. Their lips met as they kissed passionately, their tongues darting in and out of each other's mouths. She snuggled herself tightly against him while his hands explored her back and then breasts. She grasped him again. It seemed to be even harder than before.

Trevor decided he wanted put them in more a more comfortable position. He grabbed her around the waist and lifted her off the bed, then put her down on her back.

She expected him to lie on top of her so that they could kiss and fondle each other some more. Instead, he stood up, grabbed her legs, and then pulled her down the bed until her gorgeous ass was on the edge of the bed.

"What are you doing?" she asked.

He just smiled at her question. Not answering her, he knelt between her legs and spread them so that her flower was completely exposed to him. Then he put his lips on her. While his hands massaged the area around her labia, he licked the fleshy folds eagerly, sliding it up and down the slit.

Chloe trembled at the sensation, feeling her juices begin to flow. Then he pressed his mouth tighter on her labia. He sucked her clit and slid his fingers into her now very slick interior, moving them in and out. Every so often he withdrew his fingers so that he could lick her pussy lips again.

"She tastes so good, better than guacamole," he thought. He smiled briefly and the resumed licking and sucking.

Trevor continued until the juices leaking from her love canal had become so voluminous that he was sure that she was close to reaching her peak. Usually he would stop at this point and then mount her. But not this time, this time he was determined to make her birthday extra-special. He continued paying mouth attention to her.

Chloe bucked in pleasure. The hotter she became the more she moaned. "I'm almost there. Don't stop," she pleaded. She expected him to take that as a cue to stop using his mouth on her and slam inside of her. But he didn't.

After a few more minutes, she convulsed as a huge orgasm overtook her.

Uttering a very long "Ohh yes," she grabbed his head and pressed it hard against her crotch, while riding the orgasm to its conclusion.

Just as she started to come down from her sexual high, Trevor stood up, grabbed a pillow and put it under her lower back. He stood between her legs and slid his manhood into her. She was so wet with juices that he penetrated her all the way in two thrusts. He pumped into her, increasing his pace every few thrusts.

Her husband's vigorous lovemaking caused Chloe to rise back up to her peak again. Suddenly, she crashed into her second orgasm while Trevor released his hot contents into her wet center.

After a few slow in-and-out thrusts to ensure the conclusion, he fell forward onto the bed beside Chloe. They lay in each other's arms for a few moments.

After cleaning themselves in the bathroom, the loving couple got back into bed and snuggled into each other.

"That was so hot," Chloe sighed happily. "It's been a while since we've had sex this intense."

"Hmm," he agreed sleepily.

They looked at each other as if they needed to say something more. It was apparent that they were thinking the same thing.

Trevor broke the momentary silence.

"It's been a while since we've had sex this hot. Do you think our friends primed our pumps, so to speak?"

"I don't know." She replied in a whisper.

Chloe giggled, then kissed her husband. "I do know I love you, and you were great. Thank you for such a wonderful birthday present."

"You're welcome! I love you too," he replied, "And yeah, it was great!"

Chapter 7

For the first few days after Chloe's birthday, Chloe and Trevor were leery about encountering Aiko and Gerald. Much to their surprise, the couple behaved as if nothing had happened at all. They were partly relieved but also perplexed by their almost sudden return to usual neighborly behavior.

For the next three weeks, everything seemed to be back to normal. In fact, it was so normal that Chloe and Trevor began to think that Aiko and Gerald's behavior on her birthday was some kind of one-off caused by some factors entirely unknown to them.

One day, while Chloe and Trevor were talking about a variety of things, the topic of what happened on her birthday came up.

"It's almost as if we had imagined it," Trevor said to his wife. "I could have sworn they were coming on to us."

"I don't think we're deluding ourselves. Maybe they were so embarrassed by the outrageousness of their behavior that they pulled back into a shell. You know, like a turtle does when it senses danger. Maybe they were under the influence," she added.

"Under the influence of what?" he asked.

"I don't know. Maybe they had a little too much to drink before they came."

"Did you smell any alcohol on their breath?" he asked. "I certainly didn't."

"No, I didn't either," she admitted. "You and Gerald had a couple beers but that wasn't until later. Aiko and I didn't drink at all. Perhaps they smoked something," his wife ventured.

"They're non-smokers like us," he pointed out. "If they had smoked tobacco or something else, we would have smelled it on their breath or on their clothes. Besides, Gerald told me they forbid smoking of any kind in or around their home. He told me they were very strict about that."

"What other explanation is there then?" she asked. "Drugs?"

"I don't think so. They didn't seem spaced out. "From everything I've heard from them, they avoid drugs unless specifically prescribed by a doctor for something."

"Maybe we misinterpreted what we saw?" she offered.

"That's like saying we suffered from the same hallucination. I don't think so. We didn't misinterpret what we experienced. Neither of us believe that, Chloe, not really. If a woman openly flaunts her tits and smiles at the same time, where's the room for misinterpretation? You don't really believe that Gerald pressed his hard-on against you accidentally, do you? He could have avoided touching you if he really wanted to. No, I think Aiko and Gerald were actually rather brazen. They came onto us, no doubt about it."

Chloe looked perplexed. "What does that mean?" she asked.

"It means they are attracted to us. And because they were so blatant about it, I think it means they're swingers," he replied. "I think they have sex with people outside their marriage and want to involve us," he concluded.

"What the hell," she said.

"Well, it's been a few weeks since they came onto us. And they've been perfectly behaved since then. Maybe they've given up on us. Maybe it won't happen again," Trevor pointed out. "Maybe they've decided it was a one-off that didn't end well."

They fell silent for a few moments, trying to sort out their thoughts.

"They're fun to be with and they've been really nice to us too," Chloe offered. "We can still be friends with them, can't we?"

"I think so," Trevor agreed. "They're neighbors. It is always a good policy to get along with your neighbors."

"But what if they come onto us again?" she speculated. "What if they try to do something like that again?"

"Good questions, but I don't know," Trevor replied.

"How are we going to handle the situation? Break off with them?"

"I don't know," he replied frankly. "We'll cross that bridge when we get there."

* * * * *

Unknown to Chloe and Trevor, Aiko and Gerald were playing the long game. They wanted their friends to stew for a while before they stirred the pot again. They were waiting for Trevor's birthday, a little over a month after Chloe's.

As Trevor's birthday approached, Aiko stopped by to make plans with Chloe for the celebration.

"How about a barbecue?" Aiko asked Chloe. "We can use ours. I told Gerald to get the grill ready. That's his job. You can help me in the kitchen."

Chloe hesitated. The last sentence reminded her of what happened on her birthday in the kitchen.

"Sure, that sounds like a plan," Chloe finally replied. "Okay, I marinated the steaks overnight. I'll bring them over very soon."

"See you in a bit," Aiko said. "I'll leave the door unlocked. Just walk right in." Then she returned to her home.

Aiko saw Gerald working in the backyard. He had just finished setting up the grill was already ready to use it.

"Chloe is coming over," she called.

"That's nice," he called back.

"I need your help in the kitchen," she called again.

"Just a minute, I'm almost finished."

"No, now, and wash your hands."

"What's your hurry?" he asked.

"Chloe is about to come over. Get over here before she does or you'll ruin my plan."

That got Gerald's attention. After washing his hands, he joined his wife in the kitchen.

Aiko was washing dishes. Gerald noticed that she was wearing a loose fitting tee-shirt and no bra.

"What's up?" he wanted to know.

"I need you to give me a hand," she responded then giggled. "Actually, I need you to give me both hands."

He looked at her curiously.

Aiko looked out the window. Chloe was already on her way over with a tray of steaks.

"Hurry up. Get me behind me," she ordered. "Get your big manly hands under my T-shirt and play with my tits."

"But Chloe is coming now."

"Yeah, that's the point."

Suddenly, Gerald remembered that Trevor's birthday was going to be the excuse for the next step in the plot to seduce their friends into swinging. His face brightened.

"This is going to be interesting," he said.

Gerald put his hands underneath the hem of her T-shirt, ran his hands up her torso and gently grasped her breasts. He started to massage them. He loved the softness of them which contrasted sharply with the hardness of her now erect nipples sliding across his hot hands. Before long he was pressing himself against her back. He nuzzled her neck and flicked his tongue in her sensitive area behind her ear.

Gerald's attentions excited Aiko. She wiggled her butt in response causing his burgeoning hard-on to become fully erect. Her dish washing slowed down as she became increasingly distracted. "Ohh, that feels so nice," she moaned.

"Hmm," he agreed, "You want some sausage too?"

"I'd love to, hon," she replied, "But I don't want to spoil my appetite."

"I've never known you to lose your appetite for sausage," he murmured in her ear. He pressed his hard rod against her again. He was in the mood to take her right then and there, and she was in the mood to be taken.

They were beginning to enjoy themselves so much that they forgot about Chloe. Then they heard her approaching footsteps.

"She's almost here," she whispered. "Pretend we haven't noticed her. Just continue with what we're doing."

So, the couple continued fondling each other. Aiko wiggled her ass against Gerald's hard-on while he dry-humped her, massaged her breasts and nibbled on her neck.

When the horny couple came into her view, Chloe froze in place. She stood at the entrance to the kitchen with her mouth open. She put her hand to her mouth in shock. Her friends seemed not to notice her arrival. She stared at the sight of the couple in front of the kitchen sink.

Watching them turned her on. She started to fantasize what it would be like if she were in Aiko's place with Gerald draped over her back, groping and fondling her, while pressing his hard heat against her. She felt a trickle of moisture between her legs.

"Back off and get out of here," Chloe told herself. She started to back up as silently as possible.

Aiko saw the movement out the corner of her eye.

"Hi Chloe," she said suddenly, "How's it going?"

"Hi," Gerald added while still playing with his wife.

"I-I'm sorry," she stuttered. "I must have misunderstood. I thought you said it was okay for me to come over now. I'll leave you two alone."

"Please, don't go," Aiko panted as Gerald's sensual hands were still doing their magic underneath her shirt. "Stop it, hon. Chloe and I got stuff to do."

Gerald disengaged reluctantly. Knowing that Chloe was watching him put him in the mood. But he finally let go of Aiko's breasts. Her T-shirt dropped down to cover them again. Her nipples were still hard and poked out.

"I still got some work to do in the backyard." Gerald said as he smiled at Chloe, then went out the back door.

Aiko looked at Chloe. She snickered and said cheekily, "My husband is a hands-on kind of guy."

"Umm, I forgot the sauce," Chloe said looking for an excuse to leave. "Where can I put steaks for now?"

"Put them on the counter," said Aiko.

"I'm so sorry," Chloe apologized again. Then she rushed home.

"Don't worry about it," Aiko said to her as she was retreating. "Bring the sauce when you and Trevor come over."

Trevor walked up within minutes of Chloe's return home. He could tell something had happened because his wife seemed upset.

"What's up?" he asked.

"I just came from Aiko and Gerald's place. I was positive she told me to come over," she continued.

"Hold on," Trevor said. "Go slower. You've already left me behind. What happened between going there and coming back?"

"Okay," she said making an effort to slow down.

Trevor listened in silence as his wife told her tale. The more he heard, the more amazed he became.

"You're saying you are absolutely sure she said it was okay for you to come over with the steaks. Right?"

"I was sure," she confirmed. "But now I'm confused. Maybe I heard wrong," she added." I can't say I'm absolutely sure any more, but I'm pretty sure."

"But maybe not," he consoled.

"What do you mean?"

"They don't come across as dumb. I can't help but think it was deliberate."

"Deliberate?" she said in astonishment.

"Yeah, deliberate. Like I said before, I think they're coming on to us."

"But they're married," she cried. "Married people shouldn't do that."

"Sure, some do," he challenged. "But most of the time when a married person comes on to someone, they do it behind their spouse's back. What they're doing is out in the open so to speak."

"Wait, what are you trying to say?" she asked.

"I told you already, I think they're swingers," he said succinctly.

"Swingers?"

"Yeah, married people who let their partners have sexual liaisons with other people outside their marriage," he said a little exasperated, "Swappers, wife sharers, something like that."

Chloe looked at him very closely. She showed some perspicacity when she asked, "How do you know about that kind of stuff? You seem to know a lot more than me."

"I've seen that kind of stuff in porn videos."

"Ohh, you look at porn, do you?" she asked. "I'm not good enough for you."

"I mean most people watch porn at some point in life" he said. He had this awful sense that he was digging himself into an ever-deeper hole. "But that was before I married you."

Chloe looked at him suspiciously. "Do you still look at porn?"

"Very rarely, I don't have time for it anymore. Who needs porn when I have wife as sexy as you are?" This time, he was trying to assuage through flattery.

Chloe seemed to melt under his flattery. Much to his relief, she decided to drop the matter.

"Are we still going over to their place?" she asked.

While Trevor thought that flattering his wife had worked, Chloe's actual motivation not to grill him further stemmed from her own pangs of guilt for fantasizing about Gerald being on her.

"They really can't do us any harm, sweetheart, especially if we're together. As naughty as they are, I think if we pushed back enough, they'd quit."

"I think you're probably right," she agreed.

Even with Aiko and Gerald being weird, Chloe and Trevor still liked them a great deal. The older sophisticated couple's attention flattered them. Their increasingly evident mutual sexual attraction to them should have been out of bounds, taboo even, and yet it thrilled them both. In their heart of hearts, they wanted more thrills and more excitement in their lives. These unusual neighbors were too interesting, appealing, and attractive. They weren't sure, where things would lead, but they were certainly becoming curious.

Chapter 8

While Chloe and Trevor carried on their discussion at home, Gerald and Aiko were busy preparing for their friends. Gerald grilled steaks while Aiko prepared a large salad and made festive cocktails. They wondered if their friends would find some excuse to stay away.

About an hour later, Chloe and Trevor showed up to their door.

Aiko and Gerald regarded their arrival as an encouraging development in their relationship. Their advances so far had made their friends uncomfortable but had also aroused their curiosity. At this point, Gerald and Aiko thought that Chloe and Trevor were, at the very least, open to their lifestyle.

When Trevor stepped through the door, Aiko embraced him just as warmly as Gerald had when he embraced Chloe on her birthday. She knew it also turned him on. She hung on to him capturing his lips with hers.

"Happy birthday, Trevor," she said both sweetly and sincerely not releasing him from her embrace. "We're so glad we get to celebrate with you guys."

While maintaining lower body contact, she leaned her head back to look him in the eye and smiled.

"I know you told me not to buy you anything. So, I have no choice but to give you a big birthday kiss instead."

This time, she kissed him full on the lips letting her tongue slip briefly into his mouth. His hardening manhood pressing against her belly was all the evidence she needed to know her effect on him. Trevor also realized something else, Aiko was not wearing a bra. Her nipples were hard, and they pushed through their clothes against his body like pencil-points.

Another surge of desire flashed through him, causing it to stiffen more. He liked the feeling but remembered where he was, with his friends and his watching wife.

Chloe watched Aiko kiss her husband. A pang of jealousy hit her but she suppressed it. She expected something like that would happen and assumed that Gerald would do the same.

When Aiko and Trevor separated, Chloe noticed the lump in his pants. She had another bout of jealousy but then remembered her own reaction to Gerald's embrace on her birthday a few weeks ago and Trevor's forgiving attitude. She was not going to be a hypocrite. "I do not want him bringing that up," she thought. *I need to be more understanding. His reaction was, after all, a typical reaction to the sight or touch of an attractive woman, especially one that was openly showing her interest in him. It could be much worse*, she rationalized to herself. However, Chloe was still certain that he had never cheated on her.

Chloe had little chance to dwell long on Trevor's reaction to Aiko's kiss. Gerald distracted her when he took her into his arms. Although he did not kiss her, he gazed in her eyes and let his hands run down her back to below her waist where he lightly brushed the upper part of her ass. He tugged her toward him. A shiver of excitement flowed through her. Then he pulled her into him for just a few seconds, enough time for her to feel his rising. She enjoyed the touch of his hands and the warmth of his arms around her. His hardness spoke of his attraction for her and that flattered her.

After he released Chloe, Gerald led everyone to the dining room while Aiko headed for the kitchen.

"Have a seat you guys," he suggested. "It'll only take a minute or two for me to finish the steaks, if they aren't done already."

Before heading outside, he popped his head into the kitchen. "Honey, could you get Trevor a beer and something for Chloe too?"

"Yea sure. Would you like some red wine Chloe?" Aiko called from the kitchen.

"Sure," Chloe called back.

For a few minutes Trevor and Chloe were alone.

"They have such warm personalities," she told herself. "Most of the time, they make us feel really comfortable. Then at other times, just like now, they make us feel sexy and uncomfortably nervous at the same time."

Her husband interrupted her reverie. "What are you thinking, sweetie?"

"I was thinking that she turned you on, didn't she?" she said more as a statement than a question. "You can't hide it, you know." She looked at this crotch. The swelling in his pants had begun to lessen but it was still obvious.

He could not, and did not, deny it. "Yeah," he confessed out loud, "I'm sorry. But I can't control a natural reaction. Are you mad at me? Please don't be mad at me."

"No, honey, I shouldn't be," she said surprising even herself with her answer.

"And I'm guessing Gerald turned you on too," Trevor ventured to say. "I didn't see you make any real effort to pull away." He did not wait for a response. "It's kind of nice to know that a sophisticated couple like Aiko and Gerald find us attractive," Trevor offered.

"You think she's hot, don't you?" Chloe probed.

"Yeah, she is, very hot," he admitted, "But she's not as hot as you."

She looked him straight in the eyes. He seemed sincere. "Good answer," she said smiling.

He was about to ask another question when Chloe stopped him, "Gerald really is a hunk, you know." Chloe had answered the question that he about to pose.

The couple fell silent again, but a question for Gerald was percolating in Trevor's mind.

Then Gerald came back inside with the grilled steaks. "I've got the meats, honey," he called toward the kitchen with a laugh.

"Ohh wow, so corny babe. I'm coming," Aiko called back.

"Can't you wait until tonight dear?" he said, laughing at his own joke.

"You're an idiot," she said, smiling as she walked into the dining room with the salad. "Don't mind him," Aiko said.

A few minutes later, they were all eating grilled steaks, roasted potatoes and salad. Chloe was drinking red wine with Aiko while Gerald and Trevor had beers. They were having a good time and genuinely enjoying each other's company.

As they were finishing their meal, Trevor said, "Can I ask you guys a personal question?"

"Sure," Gerald said, "Anything at all."

Gerald suspected what Trevor wanted to ask him about.

Trevor hesitated. "I don't want to offend you," he began.

"We're friends man. I don't think can you ask me any questions that will offend us. Do you Aiko?" he asked turning to her.

She nodded in agreement.

"Just the same, I want to apologize in advance just in case my question really does offend you," Trevor said.

"Uh-huh, this sounds serious," Aiko said, but she was smiling when she said it.

"If it makes you feel any better," Gerald continued, "If I am offended, I promise to pretend it had never been asked. Now what's your question?"

"Are you two swingers?" he blurted out.

"Well, yes, we are." Gerald answered point-blank. "But we keep our lifestyle separate from our family, many of our friends and all the neighbors except you two. They know nothing, and we would appreciate it if you keep this to yourselves."

Even though he had suspected it, Gerald's forthrightness surprised Trevor. He fell silent, and Chloe blushed.

"Do you promise to keep it to yourselves?" Gerald asked again, needing confirmation.

Trevor and Chloe looked at each other. Then Chloe nodded in the affirmative.

"Yes, we do," Trevor replied. "Do you mind telling us more?" Trevor asked after a few moments had passed. "I mean like why, how and when you became swingers."

Chloe raised no objections, letting her husband do the questioning. But she was just as curious as he was.

Aiko decided to answer the question this time. "Well, we met a group on board a cruise ship by accident on vacation. We got trashed one night, and when they asked us to come over, we did. So, it was kinda on accident. Anyway, fast forward a few months; one day, we realized that some of the members coincidentally lived within driving distance of home. So, we decided to create a group near here."

"Ahh, those damn cruise ships. It's where all kinds of shit happen. We noticed sometimes that you had guests you didn't introduce us to." Trevor said. "And sometimes, you guys are gone for the weekend without telling us anything."

"Sometimes when we're gone for the weekend, it's because we're visiting family, our kids or other regular friends. But yes, once in a while we stay over with friends we swing with. The couples we haven't introduced you too are our from our group. We didn't want to complicate matters for either them or you. We have friends and family who know nothing about this aspect of our life. They would be appalled if they knew that we swapped partners with other like-minded couples."

"Hmm, interesting."

Over the next couple of hours, Trevor, and now Chloe, asked them a lot of questions about their lifestyle.

"We're not cheating as far as we are concerned," Aiko explained. "We don't go behind each other's backs. What we do we, we usually do together and with each other's permission. Only in special circumstances, and only when the two of us are in agreement, do we swing separately."

Suddenly, Chloe asked the question that had been nagging her since they admitted to swinging. "Why are you telling us when you don't tell anybody else in the neighborhood?"

"Ohh that's easy, we think you have the right ingredients for becoming swingers. You love each other and clearly have an honest relationship. You have outgoing personalities, the love of sex and open-mindedness."

"You see that. You see that in us? Really? Okay, well you're the swingers so I guess you would know." Chloe said as she drank her entire glass of wine in one gulp.

"Well, you kind of get a sense of these things after doing it a while."

"Okay, well, that is a lot of information, and I think we should get home. Thank you, guys, for having us over and for... 'sharing time'," Chloe said with air quotes.

"Alright. Well, let us know if you have any more questions or anything," Gerald said as they all stood up.

Aiko and Gerald expressed their birthday wishes to Trevor and Chloe once more but without the kisses and embraces. Chloe and Trevor walked home without saying a word to each other, each deep in their own thoughts.

"What the fuck!" Chloe said as soon as they closed the door to their home. "I never knew people actually did that sort of thing. I mean you read about it, but I figured it was like Big Foot or some shit."

"I've heard about it too, but I've never ever known anyone who actually did it either. I've never expected to come across people like them. I always assumed that couples who were swingers were rarer than women who don't like diamond rings."

Chloe smiled. "Babe, aren't you being a bit sexist? It's true many women like diamond rings. But there are just as many women who would rather have the money for more practical things like a down-payment on a house or a car."

"That's true," he said kissing her lightly on the lips. "I remember. You found out I was going to buy you a big rock for our engagement. You told me not to, and I really really liked that about you," he said with a hearty laugh. "You're practical about money. Our priorities match up."

"Ohh don't worry, you can buy me the big diamond later babe," she laughed. Returning to the subject at hand, she admitted, "I'm curious about it though."

"About...what?" he asked. "Learning more about what it is or doing it."

"Learning more about the lifestyle. I don't think I can do it, though."

"Yeah, I'm not too sure about it either," Trevor said in an unsure tone.

The information they received tonight from their friends surprised him. He figured Chloe would shut the whole idea down once they knew the truth. But she did not close the door to swinging.

"That's interesting. She clearly listened intently to Aiko and Gerald when they talked about their attitudes and lives as swingers. What else is she curious about?" Trevor thought.

Chapter 9

For about two weeks, Chloe and Trevor made no mention about the unusual evening they had with Aiko and Gerald. But both thought about it. They realized that, if they wanted to venture into swinging, Aiko and Gerald would be more than happy to introduce them to the lifestyle. The attractive couple had in effect proposed turning their platonic friendship into one with sexual benefits.

One night, with darkness encircling them, Chloe and Trevor were lying in bed, each thinking that the other was asleep. They separately thought the same thoughts. They wondered what it would be like to be naked in the arms of their sexy neighbors and feeling the warm touch of their bodies. Trevor got a rise as he imagined himself with his cock buried inside Aiko's petite body. Chloe imagined Gerald filling her warm interior with his rock-hard wood.

As they were facing away from each other, Chloe and Trevor simultaneously rolled over to face each other. They saw what they wanted in each other's eyes. Chloe reached for his cock and found it was already hard, while Trevor slipped his index and middle fingers into her hot wet pussy.

"Lie on your back," she said hoarsely.

As he obeyed, she lifted her leg to straddle him. She grabbed his hard rod again and aligned its head to her engorged pussy lips. She slowly impaled herself on his cock and sighed as its hardness filled her insides completely.

"Oh, sweet heart," she moaned, "I'm so horny."

"Me too," he grunted.

"Lick on my nipples. Suck them hard," she whispered.

She started riding him gently at first. Then, she sped up as the juices from her insides lubricated his pelvis. As much as they loved each other, their thoughts, and their fantasies, strayed toward Aiko and Gerald.

Trevor looked at Chloe and saw that her eyes were closed. Normally she kept them open when they made love.

"Hmm, is she thinking about Gerald?" he thought.

"Hey, are you thinking about Gerald being inside you right now?"

Chloe blushed, but she did not stop riding him. The silence to the question excited him more than he had expected. He did not stop thrusting into her. He closed his eyes and imagined that he was buried inside Aiko's body.

"It's okay, babe."

"Because you're thinking about Aiko."

"Yeah. She is riding me like there's no tomorrow. So warm and moist."

"Yeah, I bet her pussy is spitting all on your dick." Chloe said as she increased the speed.

Trevor began to thrust harder and faster.

For several minutes, they gyrated against each other.

The pulsing sensation in his cock told Trevor that his release was imminent.

"Oh god, I'm about to cum," he cried.

"Me too," she panted in agreement.

Trevor exploded. While imagining he was making love to Aiko, he jetted everything he had in his balls into Chloe's hot wet receptive interior. At the same time, Chloe's body convulsed with a huge orgasm as she imagined Gerald's cock balls-deep inside her, spraying his sticky liquid on the walls of her pussy. Then she collapsed on top of her husband.

"That was intense," Chloe declared as their mixed juices started to leak out of her and drip onto Trevor.

"Yeah, it's been a while since we've had sex that intense."

Chloe took a cloth from the box on the nearby nightstand and used it wipe up the larger gobs of their combined juices. She then went to the bathroom, followed by her husband. They both hopped in the shower, and then went to bed.

"Let's stay naked," Trevor suggested.

"Sure," Chloe said happily. She looked at her husband as she snuggled into him. "We had great sex but we did it by imagining we were in bed with other people."

"True, but don't worry. I'm still not going to cheat on you. I love only you. I still love to make love to you. Maybe, something like a little role-playing might be okay just to spice up our love lives once in a while."

He waited uncertainly for her reaction. Then she surprised him by asking, "Would you really do it with her?"

Trevor began to think that he had said the wrong thing. Uncertain where this line of questioning was heading, *damn it's got to be a trick question,* a quick thought ran through his mind. He decided to evade the question. "I told you. I won't cheat on you."

"What if I said it was okay?" she asked.

She's trying to trick me. Has to be a joke.

"I don't see how that's possible. They're a couple. They only do things together. They said so."

"Precisely," Chloe answered.

She seemed to be taking charge and in an unexpected way.

"You mean you want to..."

"Swing with them. Yes," she completed. "You're a guy. I know you think about sex with other women, especially Aiko. I believe you would never cheat on me. But I'll be honest, lots of women think about having sex with other men even when they have no intention to cheat on their husbands."

"Ah, and you're one of those women. Right?"

"Yes, I am," she said softly. "When I had my orgasm, I imagined having sex with Gerald just as you imagined having sex with Aiko. When I married you, I thought we would only have sexual thoughts about each other. Well, that's not exactly how things turned out, has it?"

They both turned to their own thoughts. A few moments of silence ensued.

"Do you actually want to swing with them?" he asked.

"Do you?" she countered.

"Yes," he said with a raspy voice.

"Me too," she replied.

That was the end of the conversation, as they kissed each other passionately. They embraced each other tightly, then went slept.

*****

Chloe was extremely nervous. Her hands were sweating, and there were butterflies in her stomach. She was trying to work up the courage to have a straightforward girl-to-girl talk with Aiko about swinging. Finally, she took a deep breath and called her friend.

"Can I come over and talk, just you and me?" she asked.

"Of course," Aiko replied. "Gerald just took the car to the shop to get it fixed. He'll be busy for a few hours. So, how about now?"

"That sounds good," she agreed. "I'll be right there."

Chloe walked over to Aiko's house. Aiko was already waiting for her at the door, and she eagerly let her friend in.

"Would you like something to drink?" she asked.

"Sure."

"Anything in particular?"

"No, whatever is easiest for you."

"How about some tea? I've got some steeping already."

"Okay." Chloe said as she leaned against the wall.

Aiko went to the kitchen to get the teapot, and returned.

"Let's go sit in the living room. Just give me a second."

Aiko pulled out two teacups and saucers from the display case and set them on the table. They sat down at the two ends of the sofa, and turned to face each other.

"Okay, I'm all-ears. What's up?" Aiko told Chloe.

"Well, Trevor and I talked about you and your lifestyle," she began with a blush on her face. Chloe was obviously nervous. "We, uhh..." her mouth went suddenly dry, "...think we might want to look into it more, maybe even try it."

"Try what exactly?" Aiko asked.

"To try swinging," she stuttered nervously, "Maybe with you guys?"

Aiko moved closer to sit beside her and took her hand.

"Don't be so nervous," she urged. "The one thing I can promise you is that nothing will be done against your will. It is an absolute rule to us that no means no. We don't make people do what they don't want to do."

Chloe looked relieved and became more relaxed, knowing the road that they were about to take had an exit ramp should they change their minds.

"So, we've already explained most of the things you need to know when we told you about our lifestyle. We belong to a local group with three other couples. We are also in contact with a swingers' group in Buffalo but distance and our otherwise busy lives mean that we see them very rarely. So, what other questions do you have right now?" she asked.

"I'm conflicted. On the one hand, it's scary. It goes against the grain of what is supposed to happen in a marriage." She hesitated. "On the other hand, the thought of having sex with some other guy is a turn-on because it's taboo, and different, and exciting."

"What does Trevor feel?" probed Aiko.

"I think he has the same feelings. I mean we talked about it."

"Hmm... it seems to me, that you two want to dip your toes in the water before you jump in. Is that a fair way of putting it?"

"Yes, actually, it's a very good way of putting it," she agreed with a laugh of relief.

"Hmm," Aiko said. She was silent for a few moments thinking about how to overcome Chloe's conundrum. Then she lit up. "I have an idea."

"What?"

"When we talked to you and Trevor, we told you that our first real swinging experience was on board a cruise ship. But we forgot to mention that we went to a swingers' club first, before we went on that cruise. There was so much to tell you about the life that we forgot to mention that particular part."

"A swingers' club," Chloe said. "That sounds like jumping into the water feet first."

"No, it wasn't like that Chloe," Aiko countered. "When we went, we agreed ahead of time to stick together and not commit ourselves to anything."

"What happened? Did you have sex with someone?" Chloe asked not giving Aiko a chance to continue.

"No and yes."

"You're not making sense Aiko."

Aiko laughed. "Just let me explain. All will become clear," she assured.

"Sorry," Chloe apologized.

"It's okay. You're just nervous. Before we went, we agreed to watch, observe and even allow physical contact, but there would be no sex. We decided to wear yellow wristbands, which, according to club rules, was supposed to convey to all those present that groping and touching was allowed, we were in a sex club after all. But it also showed we were not ready to participate in more intimate sexual activities."

Aiko laughed and then continued.

"We were actually relatively bad for first-timers. We could have worn red wristbands, which was a signal to everyone else that we were just looking and nothing more. No groping, no touching. After a while, this guy approached me and asked me to dance with him."

"Oh, wow, I'd be too nervous to go even that far."

Although the two women were alone in the house, Aiko lowered her voice and whispered to make sure that only Chloe could hear what she was about to say.

"I let him take my hand. He led me to the dance floor. The DJ was playing slow, sexy music. Other couples were on the floor, taking liberties with each other's bodies that would be frowned upon in most dance clubs. Within seconds after we began dancing, his hands were roaming all over me. His dick got really hard. He wasn't shy about pressing it against me. I was okay with all of that. To be honest he made me hot. It was exciting to have a stranger's hands probing parts of my body that only Gerald has touched since our marriage. But he wanted to take me to one of the rooms to have sex with him even though I wore a yellow band."

"If you wanted sex what color should it have been?" Chloe asked.

"Green indicated that you came for sex but it had to be a mutual agreement. So even if, say, a woman with a green wrist band is dancing with a man with a green wrist band, it does NOT, automatically mean that they will have sex with each other. Mutual consent is essential."

"Then what happened?" she asked wanting Aiko to continue her story.

"I was really nervous, and then he got aggressive. He ignored my yellow band and wanted to take me to a room and have sex with me. He scared me. I told him no. He seemed not to hear my no. At the time, I thought he had already broken two rules, asking for sex from a person wearing a yellow wristband and not taking no as an answer. Fortunately, Gerald was keeping an eye on me the whole time. He could tell I was having a problem with the guy and intervened."

"Did you report him?" Chloe asked, taking a loud sip of her tea.

"We thought about it at the time. But I also thought that I may have over-reacted. To tell you the truth, I was both very nervous and turned on. In other words, I may have sent him some mixed signals which he misinterpreted. In a swingers' club it's almost impossible to force someone to do something they don't want to do. To his credit, the guy seemed to have realized that he had made a miscalculation. He apologized profusely."

"Well shit, he must have seen your yellow wristband," Chloe objected.

"Yeah, I thought about it," Aiko conceded. "It was not impossible that he was so focussed on me that he forgot to check the color of my wristband. After his apology, I decided to let it go."

"So, that answers the 'no' part of your 'no and yes' answer," Chloe said. "What's the 'yes' part?"

Aiko laughed.

"The intensity of his attraction to me turned me on. Gerald and I went home and had great sex together." Lowering her voice, she added, "I pretended Gerald was Stan, that was the guy's name, and he pretended I was Linda, Stan's wife."

Chloe blushed.

"Why are you blushing?" Aiko asked surprised by her reaction.

Chloe broke eye contact and looked toward the ground. "After you told us about your swinging lifestyle the other day, Trevor pretended I was you and I pretended he was Gerald."

Aiko laughed as she hugged her friend. "Role-playing can be fun once in a while. We're flattered that we were able to participate in your fantasy."

Chloe giggled. "Yes, it can be. Now, what's your idea?" Chloe then asked.

"We never went back to that club because we found our swinging friends on the cruise. We've never had a reason to go back to that particular club."

Aiko paused for a few moments. "So, I think it might be a good idea for the four of us to pay a visit to that club. It'll be fun. You don't have to do anything if you don't want to. It's okay to just watch. Gerald and I will be your body guards."

"That's not a bad idea," Chloe replied. "I'll ask Trevor."

"One more thing," Aiko added, "If you decide to go, dress sexy. Don't wear a bra. No doubt you'll get some male attention. Those tits of yours will make the men drool. That's all. Having them drool about you can be a turn-on too." She winked.

Chapter 10

Two weeks later, the two couples entered the hall rented by 'The Bat in the Box' swingers club. Because it was in an industrial district, and on a Saturday night, the businesses in the area were closed. Its location also allayed Chloe's and Trevor's fears that people they knew might see them go into a swinger club. To outsiders, it was advertised as a 'Private Emotional Function.'

As they entered, Chloe chose a red wristband, giving Trevor no choice but to follow suit. He wanted to start with a yellow wristband, just like Aiko and Gerald did on their first time to the club. Still, he felt that he had to let his wife set the pace for their introduction to the lifestyle.

Aiko and Gerald, however, chose green. Both Chloe and Trevor realized that they were in for a very interesting evening. As their friends had told them, green meant that they were ready to, 'go all the way,' in the event that they found a person or persons to their sexual liking.

"You can always change to yellow or even green at any time," Aiko reminded Chloe. "Remember, even with a green wristband, you always have the right to say no. But as long as you wear red wristbands, nobody will bother you."

The two couples sat down at a table together. Aiko and Gerald had decided to stay with their friends, at least for a little while. They wanted to ensure that their friends were reasonably comfortable before they left them alone. They ordered drinks, and while they waited, the thoughts of what could happen began to fill the minds of Chloe and Trevor. They noticed about thirty couples were present. Dancing and groping were already in progress.

Chloe and Trevor were awed by the spectacle of people touching each other, intimately, without embarrassment or recrimination. They saw couples switch partners and kiss their new partners lasciviously. Men groped women's breasts and asses. In many cases, the women helped them by removing their tops and bras. Most women wore short skirts allowing their partners to slide their hands up their thighs to their warm core. The men's hand movements clearly showed that they were attempting to arouse their partners. Chloe and Trevor noticed that some women wore no panties, as their skirts were lifted.

Chloe's pussy watered at the thought of wearing no panties, and allowing Gerald to put his hand on her naked most intimate parts. She looked at her husband. His eyes were focused on the petting on the dance floor. He already had a rock hard erection. Clearly, he was turned on too.

By this time, Chloe had noticed that the women were not shy either. Some placed their hands on the bulges in the men's pants. Others were even bolder, undoing zippers and pulling out cocks, which they then stroked, slowly. Gradually the dancers shed their clothes. Although the music continued, the dancing gradually gave way to open sexual activity. Groping and touching had given way to stroking and licking. Some men were licking between the spread legs of women. Some women were sucking on the men like lollipops.

Aiko and Gerald smiled at each other as they watched their friends take in what was taking place in front of their eyes. Nothing needed to be said. The club's sexually charged atmosphere was having the desired effect on their friends' libidos. Aiko and Gerald alternated between watching the couples playing with each other on the dance floor and those who were just arriving.

For a while, all the arriving couples were strangers. Then a familiar-looking couple arrived. It dawned on Gerald who they were.

Gerald poked Aiko lightly with his elbow to get her attention. "You see that couple over there," Gerald said, flicking his head toward the front door.

"Isn't that..."

"Yes, it's the guy that came on to you when we came here the first time. The woman beside him is his wife."

"His name is Stan," she said.

"And his wife's name is Linda, I'm pretty sure," he added.

"It's them all right."

Aiko turned to Chloe. "You see that guy over there?" She said pointing at the couple Gerald had just been referring to. "The one with the paunch, black hair with silver streaks through it accompanied by the big curvy woman beside him?"

Chloe looked at the couple. They appeared to be in their fifties.

"Yes."

"He's the guy I told you about."

"That's Stan?" Chloe asked.

"Yeah."

"Are you still pissed at him Aiko?" Gerald asked.

"No, not really," she replied. "This time, I'll know how to handle the situation if it happens again. I'm not nervous this time. I won't be so touchy."

"But you can be touchy-feely, right?" Gerald said.

Aiko groaned but smiled. "Please, for once, spare me your corny jokes."

"Well, why not get the ball rolling?" Gerald suggested. "Ask him to dance with you. Get his balls rolling while you're at it."

Trevor burst out with a laugh and Chloe giggled.

Aiko turned to Chloe and rolled her eyes. "He's impossible. My husband is such a moron."

"I dare you," Gerald challenged his wife. "I'm sure he'll remember you. You're too beautiful and exotic to be forgotten."

"You're sweet and I'll take you up on your dare," Aiko answered. "You two sit tight. Watch and learn," she said addressing Chloe and Trevor.

Aiko crossed the floor. Gerald saw her ask him something. The expression on his face showed that he had just realized who he was talking to. He cast a nervous glance toward Gerald. He seemed hesitant.

Gerald decided he needed to intervene. "I'm going to leave you guys alone for a few moments. Stay here. You'll be safe. Okay?"

The couple nodded their agreement.

Gerald stood up and crossed the floor to join his wife.

"It's nice to meet you again," Gerald said, shaking Stan's hand. "Nice to see you again, too," he added addressing Linda.

"I don't think he wants to dance with me, Gerald," Aiko pouted, "Although, the way he looks at me tells me something different."

"It's okay, Stan. Dance with her. In fact, I told her to ask you."

The relief was obvious on his face. He relaxed. "Are you sure?" Stan asked Aiko.

"Yes, I'm sure," Aiko told him. "Come on. Dance with me." She grabbed Stan's hand and pulled him to the dance floor.

"Take a seat," Linda offered. "It's been a while since you two were last here."

Gerald laughed. "We've been busy. We got involved in a local group. Since then, we've been too busy to go to any club, let alone this one. Until now, that is."

"How disappointing," Linda replied sincerely. Looking toward Aiko on the dance floor, she said, "I'm sorry my husband turned you guys off so much. My husband can be an oaf sometimes but he's never forced a woman to do anything she doesn't want to do. He's actually a very decent considerate man."

"I'm glad to hear it," he replied. "I meant what I said. We've been too busy to come back."

"So, what brings you here at last?" Linda asked.

"You see that couple over there?" Gerald nodded toward Chloe and Trevor.

"The cute blonde with the handsome husband?"

"Yes, they're with us. They've asked us about the life and they're interested in exploring. This is their first time. We brought them here so that they could see what it's really about, without actually participating. Then they can decide whether or not the lifestyle is for them. So, they are very nervous."

While Gerald was talking to Linda, Chloe and Trevor's attention were focused on Aiko who was now on the dance floor with Stan. Stan's lust for her was obvious but this time she was clearly more receptive to his advances.

Aiko was determined to be her sexiest with him while putting on a show for their friends. She pasted herself against Stan. Clearly Stan's cock had already begun to harden even before their bodies made actual physical contact. She put her head down on his chest and wrapped her arms around his shoulder, leaving no doubt in Stan's mind that she was encouraging him to keep going. His rod throbbed with anticipation.

Back at Linda's table, Gerald and Linda continued their conversation while watching their spouses make out like teenagers on the dance floor.

"I remember you and your wife. I remember you skipped the red wristbands in favor of the yellow ones, which meant touching was allowed but no sex. Stan was really disappointed about that. I think he has a fetish for exotic women. That's why Stan got a little carried away."

"I surmised as much," Gerald replied. "If I may ask, has Stan ever had sex with an Asian woman?"

"That's the funny part. We've been swingers for years, but Stan has never had the opportunity to realize that particular fantasy. Aiko was the first and only chance he ever had and he blew it because of his momentary aggressiveness."

"His chances are much more realistic this time," Gerald stated.

"Really?"

"Yes, we are experienced now. Although, Aiko is not normally an exhibitionist, I suspect that she wants to put on a show for our friends' benefit. Do you mind?"

Linda laughed. "I think my husband will be the main beneficiary, and no, I don't mind. And he certainly doesn't mind, anything for a chance to bed your sweet wife."

She suddenly changed the subject. "You do know this is an on-premises event, don't you?" She added. "He'll go all the way if your wife allows it."

"I do," Gerald replied. "That's why we chose this particular night rather than a night where the fun has to be taken off-premises. We want to stimulate our friends as much as we can."

"Have you two had sex with them yet?" Linda asked.

"No," Gerald replied, "But that's our goal. It has taken us a long while to get them to this point."

While Linda and Gerald were chatting, Aiko and Stan continued dancing in a tight embrace. To encourage Stan, Aiko kissed him and let her tongue slip into his mouth. He kissed her back ardently. She felt his cock harden to its full extent.

Aiko suddenly stepped back and started unbuttoning the front of her blouse. She looked toward Chloe and Trevor to make sure they were still watching her. They were. She removed her blouse revealing that she wore no bra. When she finished undoing her buttons, the blouse hung open, partially exposing her breasts to her dancing lover.

Gerald thought that this was an excellent time to check on Chloe and Trevor. "I'll be right back, Linda. I have to check on our friends."

"Sure," she agreed.

Gerald walked back to their table. "We're going to be busy," he advised. "If you really want to know if swapping spouses is what you'd really like to do, then watch Aiko and Stan or anyone else you might care to watch. I'm going to keep company with that lady I was just talking to," he said winking at them.

Gerald returned to Linda's table. Four pairs of eyes focused on Aiko and Stan.

"Do you like what you see so far?" Aiko teased Stan.

"Oh yes," he panted, almost drooling.

"Please play with them," she told him.

Stan glanced toward Gerald, a sign of his residual nervousness about making advances on Aiko while her watchful husband was present.

Gerald nodded his approval.

"Go ahead," she said. "Play with them, please."

Stan parted her blouse to fully expose both feminine mounds. Seeing the hunger in his eyes, she said, "Please suck them. My husband wants you to suck on them. And our friends want to see you do it. I want you to suck on them. Make me feel good," she said with a tone of increasing lust in her voice.

That invitation was impossible for Stan to turn down. He took a breast in his firm right hand and sucked on it. The nipple hardened in his mouth. Aiko's response encouraged Stan to continue. He grabbed the left breast and sucked on it with more fervor than the right. He switched back and forth between them as if he could not get enough of either.

He's very good, Aiko thought. She moaned holding Stan's head to her breast as if trying to feed him. She even pushed her breast into his mouth to encourage him to suck harder.

The sight of Aiko allowing this stranger to feast on her breasts transfixed and excited both Chloe and Trevor. Chloe felt her own nipples start to harden in empathy with Aiko. She wished someone was sucking on her full, fleshy mounds, too. Trevor's cock, already stiff, imagined what it must be like to have his mouth on Aiko's female fruits.

Meanwhile, Linda and Gerald watched their spouses in the dance become increasingly worked up. Of course, they weren't the only ones.

Gerald noticed that there were mattresses spread out in various locations around the room. Some were already occupied by couples having sex. Chloe and Trevor had noticed the activity on the mattresses as well, but they were still focussed on Aiko and the man who would be her lover.

Chapter 11

Stan didn't spare a glance at the four pairs of eyes locked on him and Aiko. He didn't care. The world around them blurred into nothing, his focus sharpened to a single, undeniable truth—he needed more of her. The way she moved, the way she breathed, the heat between them—it wasn't enough. Not yet. He needed to plunge into her hot, wet depths with his aching cock. He was about to urge her to accompany him to an available mattress when he suddenly stopped, seeming to change his mind.

"Look at him," Linda laughed. "I don't think he wants to make the same mistake again by pushing too hard."

"Good, let them get worked up more. It will make their release even better and more delicious." Gerald replied.

"You're cruel," Linda laughed.

Whatever doubts Stan had seemed to vanish after a quick glance to Gerald and Linda. Seeing no objections from either of them, he led a willing Aiko to a mattress. Stan motioned to Aiko to get down on her knees. She kicked off her shoes and complied. He did likewise, facing her. Stan started to knead her breasts for a few more moments. Then he let his hands explore other parts of her body. He allowed his arms to wander down and around every curve of her exposed upper body. When he slipped his fingers under the waistband of her skirt, he discovered that she wore no panties.

"Ohh God, wow, this is about to happen," he thought.

"Take it off," Aiko urged.

Stan undid the waistband to Aiko's skirt and pulled it down to her knees. Aiko lifted one knee and then the other so that he could to remove the skirt all the way down her legs. Then he tossed it to the side. She was now completely nude. She returned to her position on her knees in front of Stan.

Stan looked crazy with desire.

"Massage her butt cheeks," Gerald called out. "She likes that."

Stan obeyed willingly. With both hands, he stroked her ass lovingly. He moved closer to her until they were chest to chest. At the same time, he lowered his lips to her neck and nibbled on it. He was careful to leave no marks, and he savored her clean natural scent. She wore no perfume. Aiko enjoyed his attention and his passion. She was now much more open to intimate physical contact with other men. She knew how eager Stan was. He was making a mighty effort to keep himself under control while pleasing her. She lifted her head off his chest to look at him.

Noticing the movement, he stopped, and without thinking, began to kiss her deeply. Aiko reciprocated with same fervent attack.

Oh wow, this man is actually a really good kisser, Aiko thought as a tingly feeling rolled through her body. *He's making me feel so hot and wet. And to think he turned me off the last time we were here.* She recognized that her attitude had evolved and that she was more receptive than she used to be.

Her hands began to explore his body, and eventually they focussed on his rock-hard dick. She gently took it into her hands. She felt a growing need to have him inside her, to give him his relief in return for her own.

Gerald was not much into voyeurism, but this time, he wanted to watch for a little while. As the foreplay between Aiko and Stan became more passionate, he looked around to find a more comfortable spot. He saw a large leather-covered armchair near the bar. Its large armrests and low plush back were perfect for what he had in mind.

He turned to Linda. "You still want to watch?"

"No, I'd rather have sex with you," she replied pointedly.

He leaned in and kissed her. "Oh, don't you worry about that," he said smiling. "Trust me. I'm looking forward to it too, but I want our shy friends to watch, if you don't mind."

Linda laughed. "No, I don't mind at all. That is what you have to expect on a night like this."

"Just give me a minute."

Gerald returned to the table where Chloe and Trevor were sitting. "We're going to be occupied for a while," he said. "We're staying in this room so that you can watch us if you want. If we don't see you when we leave, we'll assume you've gone home. If you decide that swinging is not for you, let's agree to still be friends. Okay?"

They nodded in agreement. Gerald, however, was fairly certain that they were far too curious to leave.

Gerald went back to Linda. "I told them they're on their own now." He smiled. "I want the four of us to be next to each other so that they can see us. I think they'll stay and watch. She'll probably watch us while her husband watches your husband enjoy himself with my wife."

Linda nodded her agreement. She gently interrupted the couple making out on the mattress. The amorous couple on the mattress looked up to see that Gerald was standing next to her.

"Let's go over there," Gerald suggested, pointing his finger at the empty armchair.

Aiko and Stan stopped kissing, picked up their clothes and followed Linda and Gerald to the designated spot.

Linda quickly told Stan what Gerald had in mind. Stan smiled the biggest smile of his life. He was more than happy to indulge Gerald's request because his reward would be the fulfilment of his long held fantasy of having sex with a beautiful Asian woman.

When they reached the armchair, Gerald told Aiko to sit down on the front part of the chair and lie back. She did as he said. Because she was so short, she was practically reclining in the chair.

"Spread your legs," Gerald suggested. "Let Stan see what he's been missing since the first time we were here."

As Aiko obliged them, the other three were able to see more of her smooth, creamy thighs, which seemed to act like guiderails leading to the center of her sexual being.

As Aiko spread her legs farther apart, her trimmed mound came into view. Thanks to the attention Stan had already paid to her, her labia were clearly swollen and glistened with vaginal juices. It excited her to have three sets of eyes staring at her unabashed nakedness.

* * * * *

Because people were walking back and forth, occasionally blocking their view of what was going in the armchair, Chloe and Trevor moved in closer to watch the two couples. For the first time in their lives, they saw a woman expose her genitalia in public. And this woman was their neighbor and friend. The effect on both of them was electric.

Chloe felt moisture develop between her legs. She could not imagine doing something like that; yet it thrilled her. She imagined what it must be like to be in Aiko's place. The more she thought about it, the wetter she became.

Chloe turned to look at her husband. His eyes seemed glued to Aiko's thighs and watery center. It was his first full-on view of her. He was gently stroking his cock through his pants and looked as if he were not even aware of what he was doing.

The four experienced people, however, were no longer paying any attention to the two novices watching them.

Stan was in absolute awe of Aiko. Her legs were spread and she was now completely exposed to him. At first his mouth went dry, then it began to water at the thought of eating her sweet pie.

All it will need is cream, my cream, he thought.

Gerald smiled. He knew that Stan's self-control was shredding by the second. Aiko had a strong sexual aura about her and Stan had fallen into it. Even Linda's eyes glinted as she gazed at Aiko's open wantonness. It hinted at her interest in Aiko as well.

"You want to taste?" Gerald said to Stan in invitation.

"Ohh hell, yes!" He answered.

Stan got down on his knees between Aiko's legs. He covered her with his mouth, as if he were going to swallow it whole. His tongue licked the contours of her sweet center. He lapped up her offerings, sucking, slurping and swallowing whatever spilled from inside her. He made sounds that demonstrated to anyone who might be listening he was enjoying his task. The avidity of the attention that he paid to her most intimate parts spoke to his eagerness and his devotion. The more he worked on Aiko the more vaginal juices she released for him to savor and swallow.

Gerald saw that his wife was enjoying Stan's oral ministrations. Although there were times when she preferred gentle, tender lovemaking, there were also times, like now, when she wanted her lover to be aggressive and pound her.

Gerald stepped toward the side of the armchair to have a closer look. Aiko's eyes were closed. She was panting harder as her new lover worshipped at the fleshy gates.

Gerald leaned over and kissed his wife passionately. Aiko knew her husband's kissing techniques well enough to realize who was kissing her.

"I love you, babe," he told her.

She opened her eyes, smiled and returned his kiss with equal passion. "I love you too," she whispered.

Meanwhile Stan continued his ardent exploration of Aiko's opening. Bolts of erotic energy shot through her body as one set of male lips offered her love while the other offered her lust.

Suddenly, Aiko's body convulsed in orgasm, and she squirted into Stan's mouth. He avidly swallowed most of it.

Stan was still a little worried about Gerald. His lust-filled eyes looked at Gerald as if to ask, 'what's next?'

Gerald ignored him for the moment.

"It looks like you enjoyed yourself, Aiko," Gerald stated.

"Oh, wow, did I ever!" she answered. "Stan is really good with that mouth. You kissing me at the same time was just absolutely fantastic and pushed me over the edge."

"Do you think he deserves a reward?" Gerald asked.

"Yes," she smirked, "He does."

Gerald turned to Stan. "Now's your chance to realize more of your fantasy."

Already crazed with lust, Stan took that to mean he had their permission to mount the beauty.

Stan stood up to and quickly removed all of his clothing. He then got down on his knees again between her widely spread legs. Suddenly, he stopped as if he just remembered something. He looked around and saw a bowl of condoms on a nearby table. He reached over to take one, but Aiko grabbed his arm to stop him.

"No need for that," she said almost breathlessly. "Fulfill your fantasy. Take me now. I want to feel your meat. I want you to cum in me."

"Go ahead, it's her choice," Gerald confirmed. "There's nothing she likes better than to feel the skin of a hard cock pressing against her lips. She loves to have a man squirt into her and fill her up. It's her thing, and she loves it the most."

Gerald's words caused Stan's cock to throb in eager anticipation of the prospect of seeding another man's wife.

"Isn't that true, Aiko?" Gerald asked his wife. "Nothing makes you hotter than the thought of a man painting the inside of you."

He didn't usually talk to her in such direct terms. However, he knew it would turn her on.

"It's true," she confessed.

Stan still seemed to hesitate.

"What are you waiting for? Take her, now!" Linda exclaimed.

It was an order that he was more than willing and eager to obey.

Stan dropped the condom and knee-walked to get closer to Aiko, grabbing her by the hips. He pulled her down and toward him a little so that her opening was at the same level as his cock.

He aligned his pulsating rod to her hot, seething pussy. He groaned loudly as he slowly slipped between her swollen labia. Her insides were so slick with the juices of her orgasm that her pussy offered no resistance to his penetration. He slipped into her slushy box in one easy stroke.

In most of his experiences, Gerald paid little attention to watching his wife's performances with other men, or the men's performances with her. He was usually too busy with those same men's wives.

But this time, Gerald had a close-up view of his wife's current lover thrusting his unprotected cock into her. Her pussy seemed to grasp Stan's cock. As he slid in and out of Aiko, her labia, slick with her juices and his pre-cum, seemed to disappear and reappear.

Gerald himself was not into watching, but he could understand why some men had a fetish for seeing other men possess their wives. He preferred enjoying the pleasure of another woman's flesh, while some other man was pleasuring himself with Aiko.

Stan, Gerald noticed, was struggling to control himself for fear of ejaculating too quickly into her.

For Stan, mounting this attractive Asian woman was a fantasy coming true. Filling her with his cum would be ecstasy. He had great difficulty holding back. He was too worked up to maintain a slow, consistent rhythm. The throbbing in his cock begged for immediate release.

Aiko made eye contact with him. She saw the pain of conflict in his eyes. He wanted to please her but he was also desperately in need to please himself.

"Please, it's okay," she gasped. "I'm ready for you. I need to feel you fill me up. You already took care of me once. So please, take care of yourself now."

Stan needed no further encouragement. He had already skewered her as deeply as possible. He tried to keep his meat buried deeply inside of her as he pumped her furiously. After a few moments, groaning loudly as if he were in pain, he released an enormous load into Aiko's yearning cavity.

Aiko shuddered underneath him in orgasmic bliss shortly after Stan spurted his essence into her. She was thrust up against him, wrapping her legs around him to keep him in place. Gerald guessed that she was at least still partly keyed up from the orgasm she had a few minutes ago. He anticipated that the two of them would go at it again quite soon.

When their act was completed, Stan did not withdraw from Aiko right away. He wanted to keep his cock in her relishing its feel, hoping to be ready to repeat his performance. However, as his penis deflated, their combined sexual juices began to dribble out of Aiko. Realizing that she would have to clean herself off, Stan reluctantly pulled out. The dribble turned into a flood.

* * * * *

Gerald was so entranced by the spectacle of watching Stan enthusiastically taking his wife that he momentarily forgot about his own raging hard-on and the wife of the man who was pleasuring himself with Aiko. He did not even notice that Linda had removed her clothing.

Linda spoke, breaking his focus on the two horny lovers occupying the armchair.

"I think we have a couple of problems to solve," she said.

He looked at her. "I'm sorry," he apologized. "I don't normally watch my wife have sex this intently."

Before he could muster his senses enough to ask her about what she meant by 'problems,' she added, "There's cum dripping out of your wife. We should keep this place as clean as we found it."

She took some tissue paper and handed it over to Aiko and she captured some gobs oozing out of her and then tossed the soaked tissues in the nearby garbage container.

Linda turned to Gerald. "You're the only one still wearing clothes," she complained gently. "You should take them off too."

Gerald stripped, revealing a cock standing proudly upright.

Linda looked at Aiko again. She had not moved from the position she was in when Stan had dismounted from her. She saw that more cum was about to drip out of Aiko's pussy. Her husband had clearly left a copious amount inside his newest conquest.

"Oh my, really Stan," she remarked in a chiding tone, her hands on her hips. "You shouldn't have put so much in her. Look, she's a mess. Poor thing, I guess I'd better help her clean her up."

This time Linda made no attempt to reach for the tissue paper.

"We're going to have to multitask," she declared. "I'm going to lick her clean. While I'm doing it, you're going to have to pay me back for allowing my husband to service your wife. I want you to take me from behind and load me up. If my husband can paint the inside of your wife, it's only fair that you can do it to me. No protein goes to waste on this watch."

Linda got down on her hands and knees then started to lick up and down Aiko's slit removing whatever leftovers she could find. She also stuck her tongue into Aiko's to ensure that no excess would drop out. Linda's lingual attention was also intended to keep Aiko hot and ready for Stan. She knew Stan well. In exceptional circumstances, and this was certainly an exceptional circumstance, he was capable of regaining an erection in a relatively short time.

While Linda was licking Aiko, Gerald positioned himself behind her. He stuck, first one, and then a second, finger into her vagina. Her pussy was very wet and slick. It was like a mini swamp, hot, sticky, and odorous. She was ready for him all right. Apparently, watching her husband in sexual congress with Aiko and then lapping up their shared fluids from Aiko excited her. Of course, the growing highly charged sexual atmosphere in the club, and especially seeing both Stan and Linda avidly playing with his wife, made Gerald now feel the same desperateness Stan had felt earlier. He pointed his cock at

Linda's hairy cleft. He had decided not to perform cunnilingus on her. He could tell that she was already ready to receive her lover. Instead, he pushed his fleshy sword all the way into her deliciously receptive sheath.

Initially, Gerald pumped into her slowly. Normally, he was able to control the pace of his thrusts but this time, it proved to be more difficult than usual. He slowed down to get a grip on himself and to tease the buxom woman he was pleasuring. When he thought he had better control of himself, he increased his pace a little at a time, and Linda moaned. Gerald wasn't sure whether it was because she was enjoying eating Aiko's pussy or because his rhythmic piston-like pumping was having its desire effect on her.

It was with relief that, after a few more minutes, he heard Linda's muffled gasp. "Now!"

He went in and out of her at top speed, and then blasted himself into her, jetting spurt after spurt of his seed into her welcoming sodden channel.

After waiting a few moments, Gerald disengaged himself from her. Covered in both of their juices, his cock began to shrink. Gerald grabbed a tissue, went to the washroom, and cleaned himself off. He dumped the soaked tissue into the toilet and flushed. By the time he returned, Linda had stopped licking Aiko.

Gerald looked at the two women.

"No, Aiko did not orgasm this time," Linda explained for them both, "But she is very close." She nodded toward her husband. "Stan gets turned on when he sees me lick other women. See," she said, pointing at his erect rod. "He's hard again. All I did was keep them both warmed up for the next round."

Sure enough, the sparkle of lust was back in Stan's eyes. He moved back into position between Aiko's legs. Then he seemed to change his mind. He twisted Aiko's hips to indicate what he wanted. She obliged him and flipped over onto her hands and knees, and then tipped her ass higher into the air, so that Stan could see his target more easily. He took her doggy-style, her greasy hole still slick from their last round of rutting and Linda's oral attention.

Stan took his time. He heaved into her, getting a rhythm going that he maintained for several minutes. The heat of her vaginal hole seemed to energize his manhood. When his cock twitched with eager anticipation, he stopped for a few moments, then resumed. Only when he heard Aiko moan and felt tremors reverberate through her body did he know that she had tipped over into her orgasm. Then he pumped into her hard, joining her in their mutual ecstasy as he once more flooded her channel.

Later that evening, Aiko and Gerald decided that it was time to go home. They looked around for Chloe and Trevor but noticed that they were gone.

"Maybe it was too much for them," Aiko suggested.

"Or maybe they got so hot that they decided to go home in need of some urgent relief," Gerald countered with a laugh.

"I guess we'll find out soon enough."

Chapter 12

It was late Sunday morning when the doorbell rang.

"Probably Aiko," Chloe guessed.

She opened the door. Sure enough, it was Aiko.

"May I come in?" Aiko asked.

"Of course," Chloe replied.

She led her friend to the kitchen, where she offered her a cup of coffee.

With a coffee in hand, they both sat down at the kitchen table.

"When we left last night," Aiko said, "We saw you guys had already gone." She was reluctant to mention the club explicitly because she was unsure where things stood between them.

There was a moment of silence as they sipped their coffee.

"Are you upset with me?" Aiko asked.

"No."

"Do you think I'm a slut?"

"I thought you acted like one," Chloe replied.

"Wow! Okay, listen, I make no apologies for that. I love sex and so does Gerald. We allow each other to enjoy ourselves with other people, as long as we know and agree to it."

"It wasn't quite what we expected," Chloe replied as she looked Aiko in the eyes.

"Well, what the fuck did you expect?" Aiko inquired.

"I don't know. Well, I guess I thought we were all just going to look around. I didn't expect to see you and Gerald, you know, actually do it. I guess what we expected to see was some people going off to some room and having sex in private. You guys not only did it, you did it front of everybody. And you didn't seem to care."

"You weren't wrong in your thinking," Aiko agreed. "We were just going to take you there, let you look so that you would have an idea of what it was like, and go back home with you guys. Everything changed when Linda and Stan showed up. Then, Gerald and I decided to make it real for you."

"You certainly did!" Chloe exclaimed. "But in public?"

"We don't care who's watching," Aiko answered. "Some people prefer privacy and can use rooms for that purpose. Some people love to have sex in front of other people and there are always people who love to watch. Normally, Gerald and I are neither exhibitionists nor voyeurs. Although, we are often in the same room with our lovers. What we did with Linda and Stan was intended to give you and Trevor a taste of what our lifestyle is like."

Aiko paused for a moment to give Chloe a chance to say or ask something, but she remained silent.

Aiko continued. "We do care who we're doing it with," Aiko explained. "We are usually quite particular about whom we have sex with. They have to be decent human beings that views men and women as partners and genuine equals. It's all about consenting adults sharing and enjoying sexual pleasure. But I have to apologize for not doing a better job explaining what could happen. To be honest, I genuinely thought that the chances of us actually having sex with someone there were small. After all, our first and only other visit was a disappointment. Plus, what did you actually see?" Aiko probed.

Chloe blushed. "I saw that older guy lick you and then..."

"Fuck me?" Aiko finished.

"Yes, and then you let that guy's wife lick you after he had sex with you. Are you bisexual?" Chloe asked.

Aiko thought about her question for a moment. She wanted to give a honest answer, not only to Chloe but also to herself.

"When me and Gerald first started this thing, I had never even thought about touching another woman sexually. Now, I see it as a pleasurable supplement."

Chloe looked at her questioningly.

"Foreplay followed by having a man cum in me is still my thing," Aiko explained. "Everything else is like icing on the cake."

She saw from the look on Chloe's face that she needed further explanation.

"Linda knew that Stan was not done with me yet because he has a fetish for Asian women; one that he's never had the opportunity to satisfy. So, she licked my pussy to keep me primed and to make her husband hard again while he watched. She also clearly liked to do it. Yes, she turned me on and I liked it. If she had continued, I would not have stopped her until she probably made me orgasm again. Well, you saw what happened. He took me again. It was fun."

"Yeah, I saw," Chloe conceded. "But I was really surprised when you told him not to bother with the condom. Aren't you worried about getting a disease?"

"One of our rules is that we can go bareback within our group and with the other group whose members we see once in a while. They have a similar rule. If we step outside of these two groups, we'd either have to wear a condom or get ourselves tested for STDs, which we do regularly anyway."

"How are they going to know you got tested?" She asked.

"They don't unless you ask to see the paperwork. We operate on an honor system with certain couples. Basically, we trust each other to do the right thing and observe the rules. Anyway, because we went bareback at the club, we called our doctor to arrange for a test."

"Doesn't your doctor wonder why?" Chloe asked.

"She used to, but not anymore. After a couple of tests, we decided to be straight with her and told her about our lifestyle."

"How did she react?" She asked, leaning in closer.

"Umm, surprised at first, but she said she's seen a lot of weird shit. She's pretty liberal. At the end of the day, it's just something we enjoy, consenting adults exploring what makes us happy. It's not some scandalous crime."

Changing the subject, Aiko asked. "Did you watch Gerald do Linda while she was licking me?"

"Yes." She blushed.

"Did it turn you on?"

"Yes, it did."

"Did watching Stan and me turn you on too?"

"Yes," Chloe answered without elaborating.

"Come on, tell me more. Don't be shy." Aiko urged.

Chloe hesitated.

"I've been straight with you," Aiko reminded her. "You owe me the same favor."

"Fine, okay, I'll tell you," Chloe sighed. "When I saw you under that guy, a virtual stranger, it excited me. I wondered what it would be like to be in your place, having some guy other than my husband, you know..." She stopped, obviously having difficulty getting her words out.

Aiko completed what she thought Chloe was trying to say. "You mean mount you, invade the inner sanctity of your married pussy and fill it up."

"Uhh, not exactly how I would have said it, but yes," Chloe said with a smile finally coming to her face.

"What about Trevor? How did he react? Did it turn him on?"

"Yes," she hissed.

"What turned him on? Getting new pussy or sharing yours with someone else?"

"Both," Chloe croaked. "We talked about it when we came home." She giggled. "He developed a big hard-on when he confessed that he wanted to try some strange. When I told him that he would have to share mine with other men, it seemed to turn him on even more. It was a weird convo."

"So, then why did you leave?" Aiko asked grabbing her friend's hand. "We thought you two left because you had decided that it was just too wild for you."

"If we had said no, would you stop being friends with us?" Chloe questioned.

"No, of course not. We really do like you two. We would enjoy your company without sex. We do have friends that are not about this life. To be honest, though, we would be disappointed."

"Ohh, we went home because we got super horny," Chloe confessed. "We were barely in the door when we ripped off our clothes and had sex on the living room couch. It was best sex we've had in a long time."

Aiko smiled and then said cheekily, "You could have done it in the club, you know. You could have given us a show."

Chloe blushed a deep red. "We're not ready for something that brazen," she replied softly.

"Good, they left because they were shy and horny, not because they were shocked, appalled, or disgusted," Aiko thought.

She decided not to push the issue of swapping any further, for now.

"Gerald and I are thinking of renting a cottage a couple of weekends from now. If you're free, would you be interested in joining us?" Aiko asked hopefully. "We'll enjoy each other's company as we always do. Nothing will happen if you don't want it to happen. I promise."

"That's sounds like a really good idea," Chloe replied, taking what Aiko said as reassurance. "It's been a long time since we've enjoyed nature, you know, the fresh air and the quiet nights. Well, that is except for crickets, frogs and the occasional hoot of an owl. When I was a little girl, my parents and I spent most summers in our cottage. Of course, I have to ask Trevor first. You know, before I can commit. But I think he'd like to go too."

* * * * *

Two weeks later, the two couples pulled into the driveway of the cottage around 11:00 p.m. on a Friday night. It was a moderate drive, around three hours. As soon as they turned off their cars, everything went pitch-black. It was a moonless night. They had to use their flashlights to walk the remaining steps to the cottage and unlock it. Fortunately, the cottage had all modern amenities, including lights. When they flicked them on, they saw that it was modest but nicely furnished with two bedrooms.

After taking in their supplies, hanging up their clothes and securing the cottage, the two couples decided to call it a night.

When they woke up the following morning, the sun was shining brightly. It promised to be a warm sunny day.

"Ohh look, there's a little beach over there," Chloe said excitedly pointing out the window.

"Let's make breakfast and finish our chores first," Aiko suggested. "Then we should go check it out, maybe even go swimming, if the water is warm and clean enough."

The chores took longer than expected. They decided to postpone their visit to the beach and go there after lunch instead.

The two women prepared lunch in the open kitchen. Because the temperature was already high, both women wore loose blouses and had dispensed with their bras. Chloe wore shorts while Aiko sported a short skirt, which just barely managed to cover her butt cheeks but revealed her thighs and legs.

They heard the sliding door open and close behind them.

Aiko glanced over and saw it was Gerald. He winked at her and waved his head toward the door. He indicated that she should leave and look for Trevor. The signals had been pre-arranged. She smiled. Aiko realized he was about to make a move on Chloe, and she should do the same to Trevor.

"Where are you going?" asked Chloe.

"I don't know, my stomach is feeling iffy. I'm going to the bathroom. I'll be back in a few," she replied.

Chloe shrugged her shoulders in acceptance and kept preparing lunch. As Aiko left the kitchen, Gerald approached Chloe. He walked until he was directly behind her. He leaned over her shoulder and looked at the food.

"Hmm, that looks and smells good," he said close enough to her ear that she could feel his breath.

Chloe felt a flutter of excitement course through her body. The presence of this lustful man behind her evoked the lewd memory of Gerald in the club, making love doggie-style with Linda.

"It looks good enough to eat," he added as he moved his lips closer to her neck. "In fact, you look good enough to eat. You are one sexy woman, Chloe."

Chloe was now having difficulty concentrating on the task at hand. Her nipples tingled. She felt dampness starting to form between her legs.

"Do you like me?" he whispered the question in her ear.

"I-I do. You are nice people. Nice people that do weird things," she murmured nervously.

He pressed further. "Are you attracted to me?"

"Yes, I mean, I guess so. Yeah."

"Can I touch you?"

"I think that would be okay," she responded, now completely distracted from making lunch.

Gerald inserted his hands underneath the hem of her blouse. Her warm waist tensed at the touch of his hands. He followed the contours of her body up, until he reached her generous breasts. They were larger, rounder and softer than Aiko's. He slid his hand over and around them. Her nipples became as hard as olive pits.

"Ohh!" she gasped.

"Does it feel good?" he asked, still moving his hands slowly.

"Yes," she moaned, leaning back into his chest.

"I'd love to suck on them," he whispered.

She let out a low moan as her body shivered at his touch. She imagined his mouth suckling on her nipples.

Hmm, she has extra-sensitive nipples, Gerald thought.

He kissed her on the neck and nibbled behind her ear, causing her to sigh.

Chloe felt something hard and tubular press against her ass. She moaned again. She told herself to resist his amorous fondling. Still, her body told her to capitulate to her primal desires and submit herself to the man-animal who was now clearly trying to seduce her.

Gerald finally withdrew his hands. His objective, at this point, was just to tease her. He wanted to seduce her now, but he knew that if he pushed her too hard and too fast, she might be jolted into rejecting his advances. For now, it was enough for him to turn her on. He kissed her lightly on her neck.

"I'd better let you finish lunch," he said hoarsely.

Chapter 13

While Gerald was working on seducing Trevor's luscious wife, Aiko was looking to make her move on Trevor. Still, she had not quite figured out how she would go about it. Still, she assumed Gerald must have recognized that Trevor was somehow vulnerable. "I'm going to have to fly by the seat of my panties," she giggled inwardly, "Except I'm not wearing any."

Aiko found Trevor lying on his back, his head underneath the car. Trevor had driven over some branches and had heard two loud thumps underneath his car through the driveway to the cottage. He was checking for damage.

Aiko suddenly got an idea. She squatted down and poked him on his thigh. "Hey, what are you doing?" Then she propped her hand on his thigh to catch her balance.

Trevor reacted to the sudden unexpected interruption by lifting his head and banging it against the edge of the car. "Ouch!"

"Ohh, I'm so sorry, Trevor," she said withdrawing her hand. "I didn't mean to startle you. Are you okay?"

He put his head back down.

"I think I'm going to have a bump," he replied, touching it gingerly, "But otherwise nothing serious."

She put her hand back on his thigh. Trevor turned his head and looked toward her. What he saw caused him to gape in astonishment. In front, of his face was her bare crotch. Although, he had seen her wonder box from a relative distance a couple of weeks ago at the club, now it was up close and personal. His mouth went dry at the sight of her sweetness, then it started to water as he thought about licking it.

Aiko knew she was having the desired effect on him because she saw an unmistakeable bulge develop in his shorts. The longer he looked the more his cock swelled.

"Are you sure you're okay?" She teased. "You've got another bump over here." She put her hand on it. "Yep," she said, "You definitely got another bump. Is it sore? Would you like me to kiss it and make it better?" she asked coyly.

At first, his swelling was just uncomfortable, but now it was becoming painful as the cramped space in his pants prevented his rod from assuming its natural position.

"I'll bet that hurts," she added. "It's my fault too, and I have to do something about it."

She slowly undid his belt, the waist button to his shorts and pulled down his zipper. She slipped her hand inside. Wrapping it around his now fully erect stick. She released it from its confined space, then started to stroke it.

Trevor was surprised by her forwardness. Several strokes later, he was enjoying her touch too much to object. His heart pounded at the sensuality of the moment.

"I'll check to see if there's any permanent damage," she said enjoying the feel in her hand. "It looks okay," she added a few moments later. "But just to be sure, I'll kiss it and make better."

Trevor wanted to stop her for fear of his wife catching them in a compromising position. However, he also wanted her to continue. Just as he was about to make the effort to get out from under the car, Aiko put her lips on the head of his cock and kissed it. She briefly took it in her mouth and slurped it. Then she slowly tucked it comfortably back into his underwear, and pulled up the zipper on his pants.

"Lunch should be ready now," she told him. "I don't want to spoil my appetite by having dessert first."

She stood up and walked back to the cottage. Trevor's first reaction was disappointment when both the feel of her soft hand and the sight of her sweet pussy had disappeared. He lay there for a few minutes waiting for his bulge to shrink back to its normal flaccid state. Then he moved out from beneath the car and headed toward the cottage.

While Trevor was recovering on his walk back, Aiko entered just as Gerald stepped away from Chloe. A minute later, Trevor walked inside. Gerald and Aiko winked at each other to indicate the success of their separate missions. Aiko then helped Chloe finish making lunch.

Trevor tried to be nonchalant. "What's for lunch?" He asked.

"Spicy wieners and hot buns," Gerald answered tongue in cheek. "And we've got jugs of milk to wash it down with."

Gerald and Aiko laughed heartily at his ribald humor, while Chloe and Trevor showed forced smiles.

* * * * *

The beach was a small patch of sand on the edge of a lake, it was mostly surrounded by forest. Much of the shoreline was covered in cattails. Horsetails grew in the stonier parts of the beach. The sun was bright, and temperature was hot.

Aiko thought, "Look at all those tails. And soon, I hope I'll see some man-tails too," as she noted the vegetation.

The two couples laid out their towels on patches of the beach that were relatively clear of stones.

Trevor dipped his hand into the water. "Hey, it's pretty warm."

"It should be at this time of year," Gerald remarked. "We're well into the summer. Lakes of this size tended to warm quickly after a few weeks of warm temperatures."

"Is it safe to swim here?" Chloe asked.

"No," Gerald said with a straight face, "This lake is known for its great white sharks."

"Stop teasing them," Aiko retorted.

Chloe laughed. "He's not fooling me. My parents often took me to a cottage when I was a little girl. Lakes like this have leeches, and they can be quite large. But leeches don't spread disease. If it grosses you out to have one sucking blood from you, don't swim in this lake."

"Ohh," Gerald said. "I hadn't thought about that. Yeah, I'm not going in the water."

Aiko laughed. Gerald's attempt to scare everyone had backfired.

Clearly delighted that she had caught Gerald in his own trap, Chloe continued. "Actually, it's okay to swim in the lake. It's not suitable for the creatures that the leeches usually like to feed on, like frogs and turtles, which prefer marshier conditions with tons of insects to feed on."

"Great," Aiko enthused, "We can bask in the sun and swim in the lake. The sun is high and hot. So, we don't have to worry about mosquitoes."

"But we didn't bring swimsuits," Chloe protested. "You didn't mention anything about being near a lake. I got the impression we would be in a forested area only."

"We didn't bring any swimsuits either. We can go skinny-dipping," Aiko giggled happily. "I've never done that before."

"You can't do that!" Chloe protested. "Someone might see."

"Who's to see?" Aiko pointed out. "There aren't any other cottages around here and the trees completely block the view of anyone who might be travelling down the road. They would have to deliberately drive down the driveway to see us."

It didn't take long for Aiko to stand on the beach in all her naked glory. Her blouse and skirt were on a large rock to avoid getting dirt and sand on them. Of course, there were no panties in the pile.

"Aiko, you shouldn't," Chloe protested again.

"Don't be a prude," Aiko said. "The two of you saw me naked at the club. So, what's the difference?"

They didn't respond to her question. They just looked at her with their mouths agape.

Meanwhile, Gerald removed his shorts, underwear, and piled them next to Aiko's clothes. He had removed his shirt earlier in the day. "You've seen me naked too." He added in support of his wife.

Chloe and Trevor watched as the naked couple waded into the water until they were thigh deep.

"Don't be so damn shy," Gerald called out. "Come on in."

"The water is fine," Aiko added.

Ohh, to hell with this. Chloe thought and took off her blouse. *The water is so inviting and the sun is so warm. It's been so long since I've enjoyed a weekend at the cottage. To hell with it, I'm going in.*

"Don't be a chicken," Aiko urged. Flapping her arms to imitate wings, as she made chicken sounds.

Chloe took Aiko's mocking as a challenge. After a moment's hesitation, she accepted the challenge and slipped off her shorts too, but leaving her panties.

"If you wear those in the water, we'll practically see everything anyway," Aiko called from the water.

"Ohh, she's right," Chloe thought. "I've gone this far, I might as well go all the way." She stripped off her panties quickly before she changed her mind.

Trevor was now the only clothed person. "I'll look like a real chicken if I'm the odd man out," he concluded. "Besides, Aiko has already put it in her mouth. What's left to hide?"

Trevor pulled down his shorts and underwear simultaneously.

The memory of Aiko's exposed center and her mouth on him suddenly intruded into his thoughts. He tried to suppress the memory. The last thing he wanted to do was embarrass himself with an erection in front of his wife and friends. Plus, he still hadn't gotten around to telling his wife what went down. But at the same time, he couldn't shake it off. It just kept bubbling up inside him, no matter how hard he tried to push it back.

"Ohh look, it's alive again," Aiko squealed delightedly.

That statement shocked Chloe. "Again?" She thought. *Could it be that Aiko did something with Trevor while Gerald was alone with me? It would explain the strange look on his face when he came in for lunch.*

Gerald realized that Chloe had noticed when Aiko used the word 'Again.'

"It's nice to see your gorgeous tits again too," Gerald added.

"I'll be damned, that little sneak," Trevor thought.

But, he was in no position to be angry.

Chloe and Trevor blushed at the same time. They looked at each other, but said nothing. They waded into the water, Trevor, until the water was high above his waist, and Chloe just enough to cover her generous jugs. Hiding their assets in the water relieved them of some embarrassment.

"Y'all are so shy," Gerald laughed.

Aiko and Gerald moved to join them in the deeper water.

Gerald walked past Chloe until he stood behind her. He put his hands on her breasts and drew her against his own body. Her nudity excited him. This time there was no barrier, other than the water, between his swelling meat and her well-shaped voluptuous bottom. Despite the relative coolness of the water, he could feel the heat of her naked body against it. His staff quickly became rock-hard.

As Gerald had done in the kitchen, he massaged her luscious mounds and nibbled her neck. "They're real beauties," Gerald told Trevor. "When her hands were busy making lunch, my hands were busy too."

Trevor stared at the spectacle of his friend fondling his naked wife. Although the water obscured much of the view, he saw Gerald's hands move from her breasts and then down her belly. The water obscured what Gerald was doing to his wife. Still, he had no doubt that his neighbor was still rubbing intimately.

Gerald seemed to have read his mind. He gently pushed Chloe toward the shoreline into shallower water so that her husband could see what he was doing. His hands flowed up and down her body.

Trevor noticed the signs of his wife's growing lust. Her eyes alternately opened and closed. She was panting. She was pressing against the man behind her, obviously losing herself in the sensuality of the moment. Clearly, she was enjoying his attention.

Trevor told himself that he should object but watching another man pleasure his wife caused him to start swelling.

Then he saw her move her hips from side to side, actively rubbing her ass against Gerald's hard-on. He recognized her sway as a sign that she was ready for and wanted penetration. He saw that Gerald was now totally focused on the woman in his arms and was completely ignoring him and Aiko.

Gerald reached down between their bodies to take hold of his rod. He tipped it down to get it between Chloe's thighs and then let it spring up to lodge between her legs and lips.

Trevor made no effort to stop them. He became harder when the thought flashed through his mind; Gerald was a hair away from being inside a place that only he had been since before their marriage.

He was almost sad, when Gerald and Chloe separated and headed toward the beach.

It was at precisely this moment that Aiko put her hand on Trevor's cock and stroked it. She used her other hand to cup his balls, rolling them gently. The sensation was exquisite. He could not help himself. Her hot little hand seemed to transmit its heat to his now rampant manhood.

Trevor was disappointed when Aiko released both his cock and balls. She took Trevor's hand in hers and then directed it to the hot spot between her legs.

"Please," she said simply.

He saw the urgency of lust in her face. She wanted him to touch her. He let his fingers wander over all parts of her. He stroked her labia with his fingers and touched her clitoris with a fingertip. He let his hands caress the entire area and even briefly brushed her backdoor. Then he stuck his fingers into her female channel. It was wet and hot as fire.

Chapter 14

After a few moments, Aiko released him. She took Trevor's hand and headed for the beach with him in tow. She stopped him just as they neared the shore. The water was to their knees. She dropped down and took his turgid cock in her mouth. She cupped his balls again and massaged them. He stopped, enjoying the double sensation of her hot mouth on his manhood and her little hand on his balls. He was seconds away from exploding. Then, to Trevor's chagrin, Aiko stopped.

"Let's join them for some tanning," she told him.

"What the fuck? I mean... sorry that came out harshly. Sure, let's go," he replied.

They got out of the water, dried themselves off, and took their place on a towel. None of them made any attempt to cover themselves. They spent the rest of the afternoon tanning their naked bodies on the beach.

They had aroused the younger couple, excited them and brought them to the edge, and had done it without causing any anger or irritation among them. The tipping point was approaching.

* * * * *

As the afternoon sun dipped behind the trees, casting golden streaks across the rippling lake, the two couples decided it was time to head back to the cottage—before the mosquitoes emerged from their shady hiding places, eager to feast on their bare skin.

Once inside, they made their usual rounds, checking the sliding door, the back door, and each window to ensure nothing was left open that shouldn't be. Most of the windows remained cracked, allowing the fresh evening air to drift in while the screens kept the pests at bay. Only one had to be closed, its screen torn just enough to invite unwanted guests.

"Gotta try and keep those vampires out," Gerald quipped with a smirk.

The others chuckled, the lingering warmth of the sun still tingling on their skin as they settled in for the evening.

Once they were satisfied that the cottage was mosquito-proof, they reheated leftovers from lunch for a simple supper. With the air still thick with warmth, Aiko and Gerald remained comfortably nude, and after a brief exchange of glances, Chloe and Trevor followed suit.

After cleaning up the dishes, they found themselves with an abundance of free time. The cabin was so remote that Wi-Fi wasn't even an option, leaving them completely unplugged from the outside world.

The cozy living area featured two sofas arranged in an inviting layout. One faced the fireplace, its left side angled toward the sliding door at the front of the cabin. The other sat opposite, oriented toward the glass doors, with its right side positioned near the kitchen entrance. A coffee table nestled between them, forming an 'L' shape and creating an intimate space perfect for conversation or something more.

The men finished their chores first and settled into the living area. Trevor sank into the first sofa, positioned so the coffee table rested to his right, facing the fireplace. Gerald took the right side of the second sofa, closest to the kitchen, stretching out comfortably as he waited for the women to join them.

Aiko emerged from the kitchen first, surveying the seating arrangement with a knowing smile. Without hesitation, she slid onto the couch beside Trevor. "You don't mind, do you?" she asked lightly, though she left no room for objection.

Trevor blinked, caught off guard. He had assumed Chloe would take that spot when she returned, but now Aiko was beside him, close enough that he could feel the warmth of her skin.

A minute later, Chloe stepped out of the kitchen and halted mid-stride. Her gaze landed on Aiko beside her husband, and her heart gave a nervous flutter. She arched a brow, lips parting slightly before she murmured, "Oh... okay."

A slow realization settled over her that this was no casual seating choice. This was the next step in whatever their friends had in mind.

Before Chloe had a chance to say or do anything, Gerald stood up, took her hand and pulled her toward him.

"Come here," he said, patting the empty space beside him. Seeing that Aiko was not offering to give up her space next to Trevor, she acquiesced.

Gerald knew that the four of them had to have a talk. For now, he kept his silence because in the final analysis, the wives had to be the ones making the decision whether or not they would swing. He left the initiative to Aiko.

For almost an hour the group carried on a mundane conversation about usual things.

"We all know what we really need to talk about," Aiko finally said to steer their discussion toward swinging. "Let's not pretend what happened today and even before today, didn't happen. We're good friends. Let's be honest. We are very attracted to each other."

Gerald was watching Chloe and Trevor to gauge their reaction. They were nervous but also excited by the prospect of stepping outside their marriage.

"Chloe," Aiko continued, when we were out in the lake, it was obvious to Trevor and me that you enjoyed Gerald playing with you. We saw you wiggle your ass against him. Did he get his dick inside you?" Aiko asked.

Aiko already knew the answer. Her real objective was to make Chloe recall the erotic foreplay that she had experienced a few hours ago.

"No," she answered curtly. The answer was directed more toward her husband than her friend.

"True, but I did stick my dick between her legs; so, it was close to her lips," Gerald added. "She didn't push me away. You both saw what she did."

"Out with it," Aiko urged, with a chuckle. "I know you liked his attention. "In fact, I'd bet you almost wished he had gone further. Right?"

Chloe blushed furiously.

"There's a cure for blushing." Aiko stated. "Have sex with my husband. I know you want to. We all know you want to. You're just like me, Chloe. You love cock, any cock I suspect, as long as it is attached to a man you're attracted to. In your heart of hearts, you'd like to try out a new one, wouldn't you?"

Chloe remained silent and looked awkward. Meanwhile, Gerald wrapped his left arm around Chloe's shoulder and started to play with her left breast. Her nipple began to harden from his touch and Aiko's sex talk. Trevor's cock stirred at the sight of Gerald openly playing with his wife's tits.

"I suspect," Aiko observed, "That the thought of another man pleasuring your wife turns you on."

Trevor's cock hardened more at Aiko's words. She reached over to take it in her hand. Seconds later, it stiffened to its full length.

"And the other thing that really turns you on," Aiko continued, in a sultry voice, "Is the idea of having strange pussy, like mine. You can have it if you want."

Trevor was now fully erect. The truth of Aiko's words was there for his wife and friends to see. He could not deny that he was hungry for Aiko.

"Tell your wife to give herself to my husband," Aiko pressed. "You can have me if you do."

Aiko let go of his penis. She got off the sofa and got down on her knees. She took his cock back in her hand and then put it in her mouth. She went up and down his rod with her mouth, taking most of it down her throat, repeatedly. Once in a while, she stopped at the top to lick on it.

Trevor moaned with pleasure. It felt so good. He did not want her to stop.

Gerald knew his wife well. For her, fellatio was part of the foreplay leading to the main event. As she had just said, what she liked best was to have a man's love machine pumping into her body until filling her insides.

Aiko's immediate motives were clear to Gerald. She did not want Trevor to think too much. She wanted to break down his ever-diminishing resistance, to seduce him, to make him succumb to his desires and his natural impulses. She wanted to make him lose control and ultimately make him her newest lover. She also wanted to rid Chloe of her remaining qualms about submitting herself to Gerald's sexual advances.

Now that Trevor's penis was rock-hard, Gerald expected Aiko to straddle him and envelope it within her female channel. So, he was somewhat surprised when she continued to suck on him instead. She had never allowed anyone else to cum in her mouth. Then he realized that she was slowly bringing him into the fold.

Still excited by the sexual teasing he had suffered earlier in the day, Trevor was on an exceptionally short fuse.

"Please stop, or I'll cum," he gasped.

"I think that's the point," Gerald replied, as he and Chloe watched Aiko work.

Aiko ignored him and continued. Suddenly, he heaved his hips against Aiko's face and blasted squirt after squirt down her throat. Gerald was amazed. She had not only blown him she had also swallowed.

Recovering from his orgasm, Trevor slouched in momentary ecstasy on the sofa.

Aiko snuggled up to him, taking his limp cock in her hand. She swallowed a few times to rid her tongue of his juices.

"Watch," she told him. "My husband is about to take your wife."

Aiko smiled when his cock twitched. "I won't have to wait long before he's ready again," she laughed. "I'll get my fun soon too."

Gerald realized that his wife had a triple purpose in mind. Firstly, Trevor was too sexually wound up to last. A blowjob would provide some relief and make him last much longer for the next round, which, Gerald was sure, would come very soon. Secondly, seeing her husband give into Aiko was a signal to Chloe to let loose of her own mounting passion and submit herself to Gerald's lustful advances. Lastly, it was also a signal for him to complete Chloe's initiation into swinging.

As Aiko and Trevor watched, Gerald kissed Chloe on the lips. She hesitated for a second, glancing nervously toward Trevor, before returning the kiss. But she saw that her husband was in his own kind of heaven.

Gerald kissed her again, this time more deeply. She saw no reason to resist and no longer wanted to. She reciprocated his kisses. She realized that he was a good kisser and that she was enjoying it. They continued kissing for the next few minutes, each kiss seeming to be deeper and longer.

While they kissed, Gerald filled his hands with her ample breasts. Although he was mostly an ass-and-leg man, Chloe's generous tits had a unique erotic quality all of their own.

Gerald's hands moved down Chloe's smooth flawless back until he reached her hips. "Baby-bearing hips," he thought.

Her generous thighs and ass and her fleshy genitalia evoked images of a woman who needed to be plowed, fertilized and seeded. Although he had known a number of women since he and Aiko had begun the lifestyle, none, other than Aiko herself, aroused his lust quite as quickly as Chloe did. And she was not even consciously trying to tease him.

As they continued their passionate kissing, Gerald slipped his finger into her hot erotic oven. She was soaking wet. "Trevor has one very hot wife on his hands," Gerald thought. "And, I think, he's not fully aware of it. Even Chloe doesn't realize how hot and sensual she really is."

As the minutes passed, Gerald could tell that Chloe was beginning to lose herself in her growing passions. She suddenly stood up, leading Gerald off the sofa with her. At first, he thought, she was just making it easier for his fingers to gain access to her sweet wet recesses.

"Ohh," she grunted as Gerald thrust his fingers back into her. Then she thrust her tongue deep into his mouth.

After a few more moments, Gerald pulled his fingers out of her. He let his hands flow up and down her back. He pressed his stiff manhood against her belly.

She grasped his meat.

"Lie down," she said, sounding almost urgent.

Chloe's initiative took Gerald by surprise. He had expected to have to take his time to guide her into her first extramarital adventure. She also made no attempt to take Gerald to one of the bedrooms so that they could have sex in private. She seemed willing to have her first experience in front of her husband. This also surprised him.

Gerald relaxed on the sofa resting his head on the armrest. His cock pointed straight into the air. Chloe lifted her right leg over and then positioned herself above Gerald.

"Look at how eager your wife is," Aiko told Trevor redundantly.

Even she was surprised by this turn of events. In the blink of an eye it seemed, the shy wife had transformed herself into a hot wife. Trevor was not just looking. He was staring as the fleshy gates of what had been his exclusive sexual domain lowered itself onto another man's dick. He watched her stop her downward movement just above the fleshy rod. He watched as his wife grasped the one she had ever touched since their marriage and placed its head between her moist, glistening lips. She lowered herself until his head lodged itself between her swollen labia. Then she let go of her grip and slowly impaled herself on Gerald's manhood. She gasped as his stiff member fully entered her.

"Unbelievable!" thought Trevor.

He never would have believed that his wife would give herself to another man. Yet, here she was playing an active role. The thought of sharing his wife with another man while enjoying the man's wife was a real turn-on. Despite the blowjob he had just received from Aiko, he started to throb and stiffen again.

Gerald's cock had disappeared, now completely buried inside his beautiful wife's body. She leaned over and kissed her lover again. They exchanged another passionate kiss before she sat upright again. She started grinding her pelvis against his.

"My wife has a lover now. This is some wild shit!" Trevor thought, "And she obviously wants it and loves it."

Chapter 15

Trevor had expected to feel jealous. Instead, he was thrilled. He actually wanted Gerald to take her. He wanted to share her with his neighbor. How could he possibly object after Aiko had just given him a magnificent blowjob? Trevor watched his wife's hips undulate as it slid up, down, and around on her first new rod since their marriage. She was even taking the initiative because Gerald's room for movement was relatively limited.

Of course, Gerald did not mind at all. Once in a while, he liked for a woman to take charge of their mutual pleasure.

Trevor grew heady with excitement. As he watched his wife give herself to Gerald, it occurred to him that he would probably like to see her do it again. Being screwed by another man quickly brought Trevor to a full erection.

Aiko also watched, Chloe's transformation from shy wife to sexual animal. "I knew it. She loves it as much as I do," she chortled. "The girl loves sex. She'll become a slut for you just as much as I am for Gerald."

As the minutes passed, the two lovers seemed to increase the frequency and vigor of their thrusts against each other. Chloe's hips seemed to rock back and forth, up and down, faster and faster on Gerald's column until, finally, almost begging, she suddenly yelled, "Please take me. Ohh yes, fuck me! I'm cumming!"

Her declaration was too much for Gerald. He moaned loudly as he released himself inside her hot womanhood, inundating her with his seed. Spurt after spurt shot out and splashed against the walls of her vagina, coating it.

116

While they watched their spouses heave away at each other to completion, Aiko kept her small hot hands on Trevors resurrected penis, squeezing and stroking it while they watched the sexual action on the other sofa. Trevor was ready for her. The eroticism of the situation was such that she was ready for him too.

As Chloe and Gerald untangled from each other, Aiko lay down on her back and spread her legs, inviting Trevor to enter her.

"Your turn," she declared.

With her hand still holding on, Aiko pulled him toward her eager entrance.

"Take me," she told him. "You know you want to."

Tevor gazed in her eyes. He saw the need in her face and knew that she saw his need as well. His eyes focused on her swollen mound. The thought of being in her banished all other thoughts. He settled between her legs and directed his manhood into her glistening hole. He leaned over, alternating between deep kisses and stroking her breasts while slowly pumping into her.

Aiko's ardor increased with each stroke of his penis in her body. Because Aiko had taken the edge off Trevor by giving him a blowjob, he lasted a deliciously long time as she rose to her own crescendo. As she felt her climax approach, she grabbed her lover around his shoulders and kissed him so fiercely and passionately that it caused him to unload his male essence deep inside her. As the first gush splattered her insides, Aiko joined him in a huge mutual orgasm.

Aiko and Trevor lay still for a few minutes enjoying the relaxing aftermath of their sexual union.

Aiko stirred first. She got up and headed for the bathroom.

"I'd better go before there's a line-up," she laughed, smiling at her newest lover.

Chloe, who watched her husband copulate with Aiko, was next, followed by Trevor. Finally, Gerald took his turn in the bathroom.

When Gerald joined the other three back in the main room, he noticed the time.

"Wow, time sure does fly when you're having fun," he remarked.

Aiko took Gerald's hand. "Let's go to bed."

She actually wanted to spend the night with Trevor and knew Gerald wanted to do the same with Chloe. But they also knew that their friends needed some time to talk about what they had just done. Nevertheless, they were confident that Chloe and Trevor would decide to live the life of libertines.

* * * * *

The two couples had been home for several days, and the exchange of spouses was still fresh on their minds, especially Chloe and Trevor, for whom the swap was the first time they had ever stepped outside of their monogamous state. But now, Chloe needed to talk to Aiko about their recent experiences.

Chloe had started to make some tea. She remembered what Aiko had told her about seeing her doctor to check for disease. After their adventure at the swingers' club, Aiko and Gerald had followed their own rules and had tests taken to determine whether or not they had a STD. The news had proved to be good, they were disease-free.

But their first full swing also raised other questions. Neither Aiko or Gerald were at risk of being the parent of somebody else's child. Aiko had gone through early menopause, and the risk of pregnancy really worried Chloe. She decided that a girl-to-girl talk with Aiko was needed. She phoned Aiko.

"Could we have a talk?"

"Sure, I'll come right over," Aiko replied.

As she was thinking about the things she wanted to talk about, two minutes later, the doorbell rang.

"Come on in," Chloe greeted her friend. "I was just making some tea. Would you like some?"

"Sure," Aiko replied.

"So, I have a couple of things I need to talk to you about."

Aiko nodded her agreement.

Chloe decided to start with a safe subject. "I need a family doctor, Aiko, mainly because our family needs one. Do you think your doctor would accept new patients? We've lived here for a few months now and I haven't gotten around to getting us a family doctor. It makes me nervous to be without one."

"As a matter of fact, I think she would," Aiko answered. She gave Chloe her doctor's name and address.

"Thanks. I'll call her up later today."

"So, what else did you want to talk to me about?" Aiko asked.

"Birth control."

"Birth control? What do you mean?" asked Aiko.

"I don't have any. It's another reason why I need a family doctor."

Aiko jumped in before she could continue.

"Getting pregnant is not a good idea," Aiko admonished, "Unless that is what you want. If you want more kids, stay out of the lifestyle or take some real precautions. Don't you two use condoms?"

"Trevor hates condoms. And to be honest, I don't like them either."

"What about birth control pills?" Aiko was beginning to sound like an interrogator.

"I stopped using them," Chloe explained. "They make me feel sick. So, for the last few months, we try to abstain from sex when I'm ovulating."

"Try to? Are you kidding me, Chloe?" Aiko chided. "Abstinence sucks," Aiko said. "It takes the spontaneity out of sex. It's not always reliable, especially if you're in the mood during your fertile period. Why do you think we ended up with two children?" Aiko laughed. "They weren't deliberate. We were just too horny to stop! Mind you, we did plan to have kids at some point in our lives. They just came sooner than we had expected. Don't get me wrong, though. I don't regret them. Gerald and I love them dearly." Aiko started laughing again.

"What? What's so funny?" Chloe asked.

"Despite the continued risk of a pregnancy, I can't see you guys thinking straight when you're horny." Aiko replied.

Chloe's faced turned red. "Yeah, sometimes I'm so horny I just have to have it. I've taken chances," she admitted. "Trevor tries to resist but sometimes..."

Laughing, Aiko interrupted her, "Exactly, what man has the ability to resist having sex with a hot willing woman like you?" She laughed again. "We don't have much resistance either, do we?"

"So true," Chloe agreed giggling.

When she saw that Aiko was about to continue her interrogation she exclaimed, "Aiko, please stop asking me those kinds of questions. I really need your advice."

"Sorry. Okay, okay. What is it that you need?" Aiko asked.

"I want to ask what you know about alternative methods of birth control. I was thinking about getting an IUD, but I need to consult a doctor."

"That's a possibility," Aiko agreed, and then slyly added, "There are things you can do without seeing a doctor."

"Really? What?"

"You could take him up your ass," Aiko said and then roared with laughter. "Have you tried it yet?"

Chloe blushed a deep red.

"Really, how could you say such a thing?" Chloe protested.

"I'll take that as a no," Aiko replied. "If you don't take some form of birth control, there are only two ways to prevent pregnancy, either abstinence or non-vaginal sex."

"I know, I know. When I'm fertile, I give Trevor a handjob. Sometimes, only as a treat, I give him a blowjob."

"Does he like your treats?"

"He says he does."

"Do you swallow?" Aiko asked.

"No."

"Hmm, normally, I don't either. Actually, Gerald is not all that interested in blowjobs. He says the proper place for his cum is in the uterus. When I did it at the cottage, you know, swallow Trevor's..., it was the first time I've done it in a while."

"So, why did you do it?"

"To remove his will to object to your seduction by Gerald." Aiko replied.

"Yeah, well, it obviously worked. As for anal sex, I've never done it. What about you?" Chloe asked, now curious about it.

"Only a few times, by a member of our group. He caught me off-guard, so to speak. I was both horny and a little bit drunk. It hurt a little at first. But he was gentle. It was different. It isn't something I would ask for. I guess, it's not my thing, but it is for some people."

Chloe wanted to get back to the topic of birth control.

"Come on, Aiko. Do you think an IUD would be okay? I don't know anyone with it, and you know how online forums can be. Half hated it and the other half swears by them."

"Of course, it's okay," Aiko agreed. "One of the women from the cruise had one, and she raved about the thing. They aren't for everyone, from what I understand, but I think it's good to talk with a doctor about. As long as you remember that it protects you from unwanted pregnancy but not from disease. Basically, you have to take the same precautions as we do."

"That's one of the things I'll be talking about with the doctor," she replied.

Since that conversation seemed settled, Aiko decided to change the subject.

"Have you and Trevor talked about, you know, our sexy weekend?"

"Yeah, we talked about it a few times, especially right after we came home from the cottage. He had a strange look in his eyes. I asked him why he was staring at me the way he did. Then he asked if it turned me on to have another man's cock inside me. And he got an erection as he was asking me.

Then he asked me if I liked having some other guy unload in my unprotected... I could see the excited look in his eyes. His questioning was turning me on, Aiko. I didn't get a chance to answer him. He pounced on me, and just took me. It was raw sex. I must confess; I loved it."

"Do I take that to mean you want to continue swinging?" Aiko asked, although she had already figured out what the answer would be.

"Yes," she answered simply. "We both do."

"Can I make an observation?" Aiko asked.

Chloe nodded her assent.

"Sex with someone other than one's own spouse is a huge turn-on for swingers. Variety is the spice of life. But each person is different. Gerald and I like to go bareback. I'm not capable of pregnancy anymore. So, we tend to have sex mostly within our group of swinging friends and have ourselves tested regularly."

Chloe giggled. "Well, that's not really all that kinky, Aiko, although it might be risky."

Aiko laughed. "Now look who's talking about taking risks, the lady that takes them!"

"Okay, okay, I get your point," Chloe conceded.

"Anyway," Aiko continued, "Gerald and I think Trevor has a voyeuristic streak and you have a submissive streak."

"Voyeuristic? Submissive?"

"Yes, he likes to watch you have sex with other men. He couldn't keep his eyes off you when you had sex with Gerald. In fact, it really turned him on. And you, you didn't put up any real resistance to being seduced. Only your shyness got in the way, and that will disappear very soon, if it hasn't already. So, you two are different from each other, but basically, your inclinations complement each other."

"Are you implying I'm a slut?"

Aiko smiled. "You have the potential. I think you and I are much the same. I love dick and there have been times when I've had more than one at a time. But I'm only a slut if I'm willing. Also, a 'No' from one of us during the sessions means no. Of course, Gerald's reward is his share of other women, and then he can have me," she added. "I think," Aiko continued, "You would like to be your man's slut too, as long as he's okay with it."

Chloe blushed. The rush of moisture accumulating in her vagina proved that Aiko perhaps knew her better than she knew herself.

Don't miss out!

Visit the website below and you can sign up to receive emails whenever Chad Wannamaker publishes a new book. There's no charge and no obligation.

https://books2read.com/r/B-A-NUSN-LEPQF

BOOKS 2 READ

Connecting independent readers to independent writers.

Also by Chad Wannamaker

Obsidian Tomorrow
Obsidian Tomorrow: The Storm

Pineapple Diaries of the Peach State
Pineapple Diaries of the Peach State

The new world
The New World: Series 2

Standalone
After the Midnight Hour: Murder Ward
The Winter Foursome